P9-DVT-263

The Magician's Apprentice

Kate Banks

The Magician's Apprentice

Illustrated by Peter Sís

Frances Foster Books
Farrar Straus Giroux ❋ New York

Farrar Straus Giroux Books for Young Readers
175 Fifth Avenue, New York 10010

Text copyright © 2012 by Kate Banks
Illustrations copyright © 2012 by Peter Sís
All rights reserved
Distributed in Canada by D&M Publishers, Inc.
Printed in the United States of America by
RR Donnelley and Sons, Harrisonburg, Virginia
Designed by Andrew Arnold
First edition, 2012
1   3   5   7   9   10   8   6   4   2

mackids.com

Library of Congress Cataloging-in-Publication Data
Banks, Kate, 1960–
    The magician's apprentice / Kate Banks ; pictures by Peter Sís. —
1st ed.
        p.   cm.
    Summary: When sixteen-year-old Baz becomes apprentice to a
powerful but kind magician, he makes a long journey across the
desert and into the mountains, ultimately discovering himself by
learning to dispel illusions.
    ISBN: 978-0-374-34716-1
    [1. Self-realization—Fiction.   2. Apprenticeships—Fiction.
3. Magicians—Fiction.   4. Voyages and travels—Fiction.   5. Fate and
fatalism—Fiction.   6. Fantasy.]   I. Sís, Peter, 1949–   ill.   II. Title.

PZ7.B22594Mag 2012
[Fic]—dc23

2011018297

For my teachers and guides,
with love and gratitude

The Magician's Apprentice

1

THE PROMISE HAD BEEN MADE. LIKE ANY promise it sealed a commitment, but in a golden orb of hope and expectation. In the days that followed, the promise became a sort of roaming vision to Baz, a mysterious open door, imbued with the power to propel him into the future, to see himself as something more than he was.

The stranger had appeared, it seemed, from nowhere. He wandered into the village coupled with a horse whose dark satin coat he stroked rhythmically. Every so often he would whisper in the horse's ear. Then he would smile or laugh as though they were sharing a secret or a private joke. That made Baz wonder, with a touch of envy, if the stranger could speak the language of horses, or if the horse knew the stranger's tongue.

The stranger knew his destination. He didn't hesitate but went straight to the door of Baz's home, the last in a row of dwellings built of pale mud and stone. It was nearly sunset. The day was closing its large weary eye and the light was giving way to a sleepiness that made the stranger's presence even more commanding. His sudden appearance was a subtle reminder of the very enigma of existence.

Baz sat on a low wooden stool in the courtyard, a patch of pressed earth framed by smallish trees which, at this time of day, cast shadows much larger than they themselves. He was shelling nuts, separating the meats into a woven basket. The nuts had been drying for weeks now and it was time to open them, sample their ripe fruit. Tomorrow he would take them to the market to sell. He looked forward to that. The market seemed to Baz like the pulse of life with its colorful stalls where vendors sold dyed silks and cottons, dried fruits and beans, tea, spices, and clay pots baked in the sun to a brittle hardness.

In Baz's village, as in all places where each day appeared to be the same, etched in the shadow of the day before, strangers were a welcome intrusion, arousing curiosity, and sometimes suspicion. But strangers evoked something more: the notion that the village was connected to something much larger and more meaningful, giving significance to the small square of earth that defined it.

For several hours Baz had been shelling nuts, all of them much the same: the texture of their fine, thin skins, their meats, both hard and soft at once, the little knob that projected from their round fat bellies. His fingers had fallen into a repetitive motion, finding the weakness in the tough shells, applying pressure, then extracting the nut without breaking it. It was now summer, with hot, dry days that rolled into each other indistinguishably. Baz had often found himself wishing that something would happen to break the routine. He knew it was only a matter of time before the rain would come. It always had, and the earth, like himself, was a creature of habit. But as he sat shelling nuts, he longed for it to happen sooner, bringing weeks, months of wetness, changing the dress of the world. But he knew, too, that once the rain did come, it would soon become as monotonous as the heat had been.

Baz got to his feet and rested his eyes on the flowers in the garden, their bright colors rendered more intense by the sunset. He stared defiantly, willing their petals to fall, releasing that bottled-up energy, which, like his own, longed to escape. Then he lifted his eyes and fixed them on the figure walking toward him.

In the deepest recesses of his mind, Baz had been waiting for this moment. Now that it had come it was like the rain, bringing both relief and expectation. A few years back another man had ridden into the village. He had offered to take Baz's older brother and teach him a trade. A year later his second brother had left. Baz was the last, the third son.

"Your turn will come," his mother had said as Baz watched his brothers depart with a mixture of sadness and envy at what could only be seen as opportunity. "It is in the law of threes." The law of threes had dictated his very existence on this earth, his birth, his sex. And he suspected that his mother was right. It would dictate his parting someday.

His brothers had gone willingly, eager for change.

"You will return when you've learned all there is to know." That's what the man who had taken his second brother had said. Baz had thought then that he might never see his brother again, certain that no one could glean all there was to know in a single lifetime.

* * *

The stranger left his horse in the shade of an ancient plane tree. He did not tether it but allowed it the freedom to roam. Then the stranger walked up the rough stone walkway that led to Baz's door. There was no need to knock. Baz's mother had seen the visitor and was there to greet him. She had never turned away a stranger. It was not her way, or that of her people.

"I come from the west," said the stranger. "I have been traveling since sunrise." He had come from the mountains where the land deepened in depth and color. "I am moving toward the desert." The desert was where the land faded, becoming shallower with each step.

"Please come in and have tea with us," said Baz's mother, opening the door ever wider. Baz bowed slightly before the man, his elder. Then his father appeared and took the stranger's hands, as was their custom. "Welcome," he said.

The house smelled of dried spice, of tallow for soap and candles, of familiarity to Baz. He knew that the visitor would inhale this familiarity not with the same value or attachment that he did, but with an otherness, a newness. This made him sorry in a way. And as he tried to follow the stranger's gaze he saw his own surroundings differently, acutely aware of how perceptions were formed by habit. The rough woven cloth on the walls, the humble wooden objects his father had carved that lined the shelves, even the odor of nut oil rubbed into his skin, became foreign, strange, and otherly.

The white walls and beige tiled floor guarded the coolness of days, of time passed. But the fiery red cushions huddled comfortably around a low wooden table spoke of warmth and welcome.

The stranger seated himself across from Baz, folding his legs and placing his palms on his knees. Baz's mother brought the tea, a blend of jasmine and rose leaves, and a plate of sugary sweets. Then she took her place to the left of her son.

The visitor stroked a scarf wound loosely around his neck. His tunic with its wide bands of red, blue, and orange meant that he probably belonged to some tribe. Its loose weave and color made him look almost comical. He had come from afar. In Baz's village, they dressed in finely woven ivory, white, and beige, tones that reflected the sun. Only when the rains came did they don darker shades.

The stranger sipped his tea slowly, savoring each mouthful, rolling the hot liquid from one cheek to the other like a tiny ball. He picked delicately at the plate of sweets, playfully popping them into his mouth.

"Ahh," he sighed, satisfied. Then his eyes settled on Baz's father, who was refilling the cups of tea and whose hands gave away his trade. He was a craftsman, a wood-carver, but he was slowly losing his sight and feared that he wouldn't be able to work much longer. The stranger's gaze moved into the distance, to the room at the end of the house where Baz's father turned his creations. His father knew that this was the work he had been born for, and he settled into it each day with quiet dignity. In that room he felt a oneness that linked him to his creations, and to all that was. But he knew, too, that this work was not for his sons. He was as sure of it as he was that the rising sun was bound to set.

The stranger did not introduce himself but got right to the point of his visit. "I have come from Kallah, a weaving town," he said in a booming voice. "Surely you have heard of it," he added, slowing his words, nearly whispering. He was like a bard telling a tale, imbuing each syllable, each phrase, with suspense. He waved his hands in the air, another gesture that told Baz that this man was from afar. The people in Baz's village were more subdued, discreet. Without thinking, Baz let his eyes fall on the man's hands, which now cradled the teacup. They were large, with long graceful fingers, but the nails were hard-looking, framed in a thin line of dirt that traced the edges of his fingertips.

Suddenly the stranger put down his teacup and reached across the table. "So who have we here?" he said.

"I'm Baz," said the boy.

The stranger held Baz's hands in his own like a treasure. "There is always a need for young hands like these," he said. Then he tilted his head to one side. "Somewhat soft," he said, smiling. His teeth were pearly white and his gums pink. "But agile and nimble. Not the hands of a wood-carver, I'm afraid, but the hands of a weaver, yes."

The stranger released Baz's hands, then reached for his tea. He was practiced in the art of persuasion and knew that he must allow time for his words to settle into the minds and hearts of his audience. He already knew the answer to what he was about to suggest, but he waited patiently, making the proposal in due time.

"You, my boy, will be an apprentice to one of the greatest weavers in Kallah." He turned to Baz's mother and father. "He will learn the trade in return for his keep. Then in some future time he will be free to continue, in a superior role." The stranger paused. "Or return home," he said carelessly, the tone of his voice suggesting that Baz would never do that. The stranger turned to Baz. "As he wishes." Then he distanced himself, his eyes following the rays of light that had burst through the window, creating a pattern of dancing stripes across the floor.

"Do you wish to go, son?" Baz's father asked.

Baz did not have to think or reflect. He knew the answer as well as he knew his name.

"Yes," he said.

So the promise was made, and sealed in a show of clasped hands, his mother's small and soft, his father's square and rough, Baz's own long and nimble, and those of the stranger tinged with dirt.

"I will continue my journey," said the stranger, getting to his feet. "But I will return before the new moon."

Baz led the stranger out to where his horse was waiting next to the plane tree. "What is your name?" he asked.

"I do not have one name," said the stranger, frowning. "People call me many things. What would you call me?"

Baz did not have to think long. "You are the Man Who Loves His Horse," he said.

This made the stranger smile.

❀　❀　❀

Baz reviewed his life, all sixteen years of it, with the sweet nostalgia that always comes before a parting. A film of dust settled like a pastel haze, covering any unpleasantness. He thought of the departure of his two brothers who had yet to return.

"I'll be back," he said to his mother. He repeated these same words many times to himself as if the repetition of the phrase would ensure its coming to pass.

"Of course you will," said his mother, hanging the washed clothes in the sun to dry. They were worn to a comfort much like Baz's own life.

In his mother's gaze Baz saw the soul of a woman who was seeing her child for the last time. Despite that, Baz did not think for a moment that he wouldn't go, nor did his parents, who shared the knowledge that they were doing what was right. They knew not where this came from. They could barely describe it beyond the feeling that sometimes in life certain things were meant to be. And this was one of them.

"Maybe the stranger won't return," said Baz's mother with a half smile.

Baz breathed in her scent, a mixture of smells coupled with sounds. In the corner sat an instrument that she played, some strings attached to a wooden frame. Baz had no idea where it had come from, only that it was something she'd always had, one of those things with no discernible origins, no real beginnings. It was simply there, a part of her.

"Maybe," said Baz, smiling back at her, attempting to build suspense into an event that had none because they all knew the truth. The stranger would return.

❋　❋　❋

As Baz prepared for bed he lit a candle and watched the flame begin to flicker, mirroring the agitation he felt inside. He tried to stop it with his eyes, but it jumped even higher until he gave up.

He drifted into sleep, dreaming of water. A man appeared who wished to buy him. The man was smiling. But then the water rose, engulfing the image. And the night that had seemed so long when it lay ahead was suddenly over. The following days flew, too, until it seemed there were mere minutes between one moon and the next.

2

THE STRANGER RETURNED WEARY FROM THE heat and travel. The bright colors of his tunic had faded, melting together like those of a sunset, and his skin had turned dark.

"Have you not been home?" Baz's mother asked.

"I do not have a home. I am but a messenger," said the stranger. "The world is my home." Then his voice dropped and his face became somber. "I have a message for you," he said.

"For me?" said Baz, puzzled.

"You will follow the light," he said.

"The light?" said Baz.

The stranger shrugged. "The birds, the trees, and the wind all tell me. My horse tells me. So I know it must be true."

Baz had no idea what the stranger was talking about, so for the time being he pushed his questions to the back of his mind.

❋ ❋ ❋

Baz had tried to keep the moment of parting far from his thoughts, which leaped fleetingly back and forth between past and future. But when that time arrived, he wished to stay anchored in the moment where there was nothing but the present, his loving parents, and possibility.

"Goodbye, Baz," said his mother, hugging him.

"Good luck and good fortune, son," said his father, embracing his child.

Then it was over and Baz was traveling, seated on the back of a horse behind a stranger, distancing himself from all that he knew.

He carried a small sack laden with fresh tunics, heavy and light, trousers, leggings, and socks. He had stuffed his pockets with dried fruit, nuts, and tea, along with a wooden carving from his father, a small silver drinking vessel from his mother, and the few coins he'd saved. It wasn't long before he noticed that if he held the feeling of those objects—love and familiarity—while looking at something else, maybe a tree, or the sky, then those feelings would be re-created in that object. This was like magic to Baz. He wondered if others could do the same, and longed to ask the stranger. But the stranger seemed lost in his own thoughts, chewing on tobacco or something else, which had a foul smell and caused the saliva in his mouth to mount so that he had to spit frequently. When the stranger turned his head and parted his lips Baz caught a glimpse of his straight white teeth, which in a funny way reminded him of the tight rows of white houses he'd just left behind.

* * *

At first, they passed through villages much like Baz's own. Every so often the stranger would lean toward his horse and whisper in its ear.

"Does your horse have a name?" Baz asked.

"Melesh," said the stranger.

"Melesh," repeated Baz, leaning back to pet the horse's solid flank.

Baz watched the world pass. The colors of his own home began to fade into pale fields of wheat, yellow mustard, and sunflowers with their heads bent skyward. His mind wandered back to the stranger's message and he wondered how these plants could know more than he did.

When dusk fell they climbed down from the horse and continued on foot. The ground was dry, but a patch of pink and blue flowers had pushed through the stiff earth. Baz watched as the stranger, unaware, stepped on them with his heavy tread, flattening them. But their color resisted, looking more like a brushed sunset than ever.

"You must be hungry," the stranger said. He had stopped to give Melesh water. Then he lifted his tunic. Underneath, colored sacks of provisions were sewn into the lining. He looked funny to Baz, like a traveling tradesman exhibiting his wares.

"I've brought some food, too," said Baz, reaching into his own pockets.

The stranger held up a broad hand in protest. "No, no," he said. "You must keep that for later." He offered Baz some seeds, flatbread, and dried fruit. Then they drank water from a gourd.

At night they slept on a thick woven blanket laid out on the ground. Baz had always had something soft under him or next to him. This hardness was new and at first he resisted it, but then his tired body gave way and he sank into blissful slumber.

In the days that followed, the growth around them became sparser, stubbier, replaced by succulents that oozed a thick, clear, viscous fluid that the stranger would rub into his dry skin. At the beginning of their journey, Baz tried to remember the route, the landmarks, drawing a map in his mind for the day he would return home. But when the detail became too much he began to think of his journey in other ways.

"I am two sunrises and two sunsets from home," he would tell himself. "I am fourteen cacti, two enormous fields of mustard, four new colors away from home."

Baz began to see the sunrise differently. Although he knew it was the same, he marveled at the way it looked from each new position on the earth. Objects he saw for the first time he viewed with no attachment. He enjoyed this feeling of neutrality that showed him that the meaning of life is not in its objects.

Far into the distance, Baz could see the shadow of the mountains turn from violet to blue. At night they seemed to creep closer as though they plowed through the earth on invisible feet. Then as the light returned they would retreat again and the scenery would change. As the days passed the vast fields of mustard turned from deep yellow to bright red.

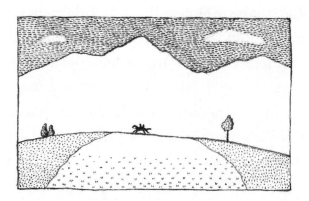

"That is madder," said the stranger. "It's for making dye for cloth and carpets. It will soon become part of you."

This was the first time that the stranger had mentioned the work that Baz would do.

"And beyond those fields?" Baz asked.

"That is our destination," said the stranger. "Kallah."

Kallah was more than a day's ride away, so the stranger chose to stop in the next village they came to, a cluster of stout mud and stone houses. Their low ceilings reminded Baz of how the earth could move in strange and violent ways, and how that movement had become embedded in the consciousness of the people, in their way of life. Any day the earth might shift under their feet, turning their world upside down.

The stranger went to the nearest inn and put Melesh in the stable to feed. Then he took a tiny room with two mattresses rolled out across the floor, and a washbasin. A window opened toward the west and another toward the east.

They dined next to the kitchen at a long, narrow wooden table with fellow travelers.

"They are seekers," whispered the stranger.

"Seekers?" asked Baz. "What are they searching for?"

The stranger chuckled. "Fortune, happiness, wealth, truth, knowledge, wisdom, love, beauty," he said, his voice growing louder.

A man sitting to the left of Baz reached out and twitched Baz's ear affectionately. Baz looked at his face, marked with ugly moles, and tried to grow accustomed to the sight. But it refused to make itself familiar like other things did, no matter how much Baz wished it to.

"And what are you seeking, young man?" the man

asked Baz, sucking in his breath in eager anticipation of the boy's answer.

"I am seeking work," said Baz.

"Ahh." The ugly man nodded. "I am seeking beauty," he said. "But I never move from this bench."

"It's true," said another. "He sits day in, day out and contemplates the room and everything in it."

"All homely, as I am," said the man. "But I wait for the day when that will change and all will be beautiful before my eyes." He grinned and the others at the table laughed at the improbability of this. But the ugly man continued to smile.

"Not only ugly but stupid," said someone at the end of the table. He was staring gleefully into a bowl of mango paste where a small fly struggled to free itself. "Now that's a pretty sight," he added. And suddenly, urged on by an uncontrollable impulse, he pinched the fly between his finger and thumb and flicked it into a corner. "Now survival is up to him," he said smugly.

The innkeeper arrived with plates of curried lentils, chickpeas, steaming flatbreads, which the travelers washed down with wine of a deep red color like the fields of madder. Then they sucked on tiny cubes of sugared ginger that made Baz's mouth water.

Baz was not accustomed to wine, so he drank a sweet drink of cardamom pods, anise, and honey instead. The ugly man with the moles abstained from the wine, too.

"It would distract me from my objective, which is beauty," he said, leaning back and contemplating the table.

The stranger filled his glass with wine again and again, becoming merrier with each round. When at last he rose from the table, his gait was crooked. His face had darkened in color, but his brown eyes with their hazel flecks glowed like amber in a fire.

"Good night, my fellow travelers," he said, beckoning for Baz to join him.

Baz lowered his eyes and nodded to the others. He had always been taught that there was something to learn from his elders. He was deciding now if that had to do with seeking beauty or drowning in drink.

The stranger had some sugar for Melesh, so Baz followed him to the stable. He began to sing sweetly, and although Baz did not know the melody, he followed the soft round notes. The stranger's voice was like his hands, fine and gentle. It sounded beautiful to Baz.

"Oh, Melesh," sang the stranger. Then he sighed, letting out a breath that reeked of liquor. He lifted his hand to the horse's mouth and Melesh lapped up the sugar eagerly, asking for more.

"No, no," said the stranger. "That is all." His eyebrows slanted downward, frowning. Baz, too, felt sorry for the horse, recognizing the feeling of desire only partially filled. Then the stranger began to whisper in the horse's ear. Melesh shivered and Baz wondered what the horse had been told. He waited for the stranger to continue, but instead he dropped to the floor, closing his eyes. He lay there, still, for several minutes, but then he opened his eyes and propped himself on an elbow, beckoning to Baz.

Baz leaned down until he felt the stranger's hot sour breath close to his skin, but the stranger dropped back onto the floor and buried his head in the hay. He closed his eyes and soon fell fast asleep.

Baz moved close to Melesh and patted his mane. But the horse just looked at him sleepily. Baz did not want to wake the stranger. Nor did he wish to leave him. So he arranged the hay in a small oval beside the horse and lay down, the small room with the mattresses a distant memory of softness and comfort. Under his body he felt the earth rumble.

3

BAZ AWOKE EARLY. HE WAS DEBATING WHETH-
er or not he should rouse the stranger, who was
still sound asleep. But then Melesh made the deci-
sion, stepping forward to nuzzle his keeper into
wakefulness.

The stranger groaned but reached out to pet the
horse. Then he stumbled to his feet.

"I've paid for a room and slept in the stable," he

said, annoyed with himself. Baz waited to be blamed, but the stranger did not fault him. Instead, he took a brush from under his tunic and swept it across Melesh's coat. With each stroke, his chagrin lessened. Then he handed the brush to Baz and went off to wash.

The long wooden table had been cleared from the night before and there were no signs of their fellow travelers. Even the ugly man with the moles must have either triumphed in his quest for beauty or given it up altogether. The table was set with tea and plates of bread, butter, and honey. The stranger ate ravenously, squirreling away several lumps of brown sugar for Melesh. He winked at Baz to do the same. Then they replenished their drinking vessels and set off again.

It was late afternoon when they reached the outskirts of Kallah. Rows of houses spread out around a thick center, much like a flower with its petals.

The stranger found a shady spot for Melesh under

an overhanging roof. Then he entered a tiny passage-way that still managed to attract a single ray of light that sliced across the wall.

"This way," he said.

Baz followed the stranger into a small, untidy garden ripe with the flowers of summer—roses, jasmine, dahlias. There were vegetables, too—cucumbers and radishes, okra and tomatoes—which thinned out, gradually giving way to a row of wooden buildings.

Behind the buildings was another corridor lit-tered with chipped ceramic bowls, dented tin pots and pans, a few wooden stools, splintered and cracked. To Baz they were the first signs of a broken dream. At the end was a booth that housed a man perched on a tall stool, spinning a revolver around his index finger. When he saw them coming, he slipped the gun into a drawer and hurried to greet the stranger, planting a kiss on either cheek. Then he turned to Baz.

"Let us see," he said, tapping a dirty bitten-down fingernail against a gold tooth on one side of his mouth. He reached for Baz's hands and studied them, allowing the agile fingers to rest in his own fat, stubby grip.

"This is your master," the stranger said to Baz.

Baz lowered his head and nodded humbly. "I am Baz," he said.

"Baz." The man repeated his name twice, thrice. Then he pulled the stranger aside and gripped his elbow firmly. They spoke in hushed voices for several minutes while Baz turned in a small arc, widening

his gaze to take in his surroundings, a group of di-
sheveled wooden buildings leaning against one another for support, and an empty courtyard with a
dirt floor. Not far from the booth was a pile of dog
excrement swarming with flies. Baz rested his eyes
on it for several seconds, then turned back to the
stranger, who was now at his side.

"Good luck and good fortune," he said, kissing
Baz on each cheek.

"Where will you go?" asked Baz, who felt he had
a right to know the destination of this stranger
who had played a part in his destiny.

But the stranger did not answer him. "I have kept
my promise," he said. "Here you will learn to weave."

❋ ❋ ❋

That evening Baz found himself sitting on another
long wooden bench among strangers. These were not
travelers, but young men like himself.

"My disciples," said the master, barely able to say the word. "This is Baz." He laughed and the boys lowered their heads without speaking. Most of them looked older than Baz, but across from him sat a boy whom Baz guessed to be more or less his age. He was tall but very thin with hair and eyes as dark as night. His face was beautiful and for some reason that brought to Baz's mind the image of the ugly man with the moles.

Dinner was mashed chickpeas with raw garlic served in unwashed, chipped bowls. It was so strong that it burned Baz's tongue. There was a tin cup of water for each of them, which reflected back the sad, weary faces of the table's occupants.

When they'd finished eating, the master rose and circled the table with a basin of muddy water. Baz dropped his bowl and cup in, listening to them clank against each other. Then the master led them from the table to the stables, where there was an old cement trough half-filled with water.

"For washing," said the master, eyeing Baz. Then he spread his arms wide like the hands of a clock and turned in a circle. "For sleep," he said. "The choice is yours."

The stable had no animals other than a little dog napping on one of the mounds of hay that burgeoned from the ground. He raised his head at the sound of the master's voice, but did not move from his perch.

Baz waited for the other boys to take their places, then chose what was left, the mound closest to the door. After he had knelt down and spread the hay evenly the master handed him a small tin box for his possessions.

"Best you hang on to it," he said.

Baz began to put the few things from his sack into the box, but then caught the boy with the dark eyes shaking his head.

"Don't you have a box?" whispered Baz.

"I did once," answered the boy. "But it disappeared."

"No talking. You'll wake the mules next door," said the master, laughing. Then he took a whip and swatted the ground, causing the dust to rise in tiny smokelike coils.

Baz rinsed himself in the trough. The water was warm but grainy with dirt. Still, Baz liked the feel of it against his skin. Then he returned to his mound of hay. The other boys were already sleeping. Baz knew by now that if he tried to imagine what awaited him he would never sleep. Or if he did manage to sleep he might never wake. So he fixed his vision on a single shaft of grain rising from the floor. He stared into it until it seemed to expand before his eyes. Then he blinked and it returned to its original form. At some point Baz heard distant voices, but he wasn't sure if they were real or in his own head. At last the voices ceased, and he felt his body give way to sleep.

❀   ❀   ❀

"Get up, get up," cried the master. Baz felt a stick poke into his side.

The master prodded each of them, then stood tapping the stick on the ground while they washed and dressed. The boy with the dark eyes offered Baz a sliver of soap. "I'm Dagar," he said.

"Thank you," said Baz, taking the soap, squeezing it in his fist, acutely aware of its worth. "Dagar," he repeated, realizing how a name gave identity to something or someone that had none. "And I'm Baz," he whispered. "How long have you been here?"

"I don't know," said Dagar. "Months, years. I don't even know how old I am anymore."

"Did they promise you could go home?" asked Baz.

Dagar nodded. "My first master did. But he is no longer here."

Baz was about to ask what happened to him when a whip thrashed, cutting through their quiet chatter.

"The silencer is at work," said the master, referring to his whip. "And you should be, too."

He led them to the wooden table, still dirty with traces of the previous evening's meal, and offered each of them a slice of stale bread. A small pot of crystallized honey sat in the middle of the table drawing flies.

"Uninvited guests," the master cried as he swung the whip again, dispersing the flies.

Baz reached forward with his spoon, his eye on the whip. He measured the seconds it took to rise, then fall. Then he dipped his spoon into the honey. But he wasn't quick enough and the whip landed on the back of his hand. Baz dropped the spoon and watched the skin crack open, counting the time it took for the numbness to pass and the pain to set in. The heat from the welt merged with an inner heat born from somewhere deep inside.

Suddenly, the master handed Baz his spoon dripping with honey.

Baz hesitated, wondering if he should take it. Slowly he reached for the spoon. The master loosened his grip on it, letting it go.

"Bravery is to be honored," he said.

❊ ❊ ❊

The weaving took place in a small courtyard covered with a thin canvas awning to keep out the sun. Baz was taught not by the master but by Dagar, who patiently showed him how to make knots in the threads.

"He knows nothing about weaving," whispered Dagar. "I learned from the master who was here before him."

Baz repeated the movements. He was a quick learner, soon becoming adept at the knots while the master walked in circles with his whip, letting it fly each time one of his workers slowed his pace.

"How do I know when it is time to change colors?" asked Baz.

"Watch me and soon it will come to you," said Dagar, quietly measuring his words because the master was watching.

Before long Baz was weaving the patterns all on his own. Sometimes the little dog from the stable would trot into the courtyard and sit patiently watching the boys work. Then he would run in a circle chasing his own tail, and Baz would marvel how he was able to amuse himself with such a small thing.

* * *

"What do you think about as you weave?" Baz asked Dagar one day.

"My family," said Dagar. "Sometimes it seems that I am weaving them into my carpets. But then I am afraid people won't buy them because they are sad."

"Why did you come here?" asked Baz.

"We are five, my brothers and sisters and me. My father is a farmer, but our land is too small to be divided among us. So when the old master came looking for a boy to weave I stepped forward. I have the hands for it," he said, sighing.

It was true. Baz had not been there long, but he saw that Dagar was a gifted weaver who worked beautiful designs.

"And you?" asked Dagar.

"A stranger came to my village one day. My brothers had left to learn a trade. And I knew that I must, too. So I followed him. And here I am." Baz felt the blood rising, pulsating in his temples. "But someday I will return home."

"When I first came here I liked it," said Dagar. "The old master was kind. Not like this one." Dagar reached beneath his tunic and pulled out a square of tapestry rolled into a tight cylinder. He opened it for Baz to see.

Baz studied figures—plants, animals, the stars, the sun, and the moon—all woven together in a finely wrought dance. He had never seen anything so beautiful. The longer he looked the more it seemed that the tapestry came to life.

"The old master gave this to me," said Dagar.

"What happened to him?" asked Baz.

Dagar shook his head. "I don't know," he said. "He became ill, and then one morning when we awoke, the new master was there to greet us with the whip. Then I began to work faster, because I thought the quicker I worked, the sooner I would be able to leave. But this master will never let me go. He says I am made for this kind of work." Dagar looked down at his thin arms and legs doubtfully. "I've become nothing but a thread myself," he said, rolling the tapestry and tucking it back under his tunic. He smiled, but a deep sadness rimmed his eyes.

Dagar drank from his tin cup, then shared the rest with the little dog, who had crossed the courtyard and was rubbing up against Dagar's legs.

"I call him Blink," said Dagar. "See how he blinks his eyes? It's the dirt and dust. I don't know where he came from but I consider him mine. There is nothing else around here that is mine. I'm not even mine."

Baz smiled. "I guess none of us are," he said.

Suddenly Blink was standing behind Baz, wagging his tail. Baz reached down to pet the dog. "Come," he said just before the whip bit into his spine.

"Playtime is over," shouted the master. "There's work to be done."

Baz returned to his weaving. But he felt the whip

crawling up his back, burning into the layers of flesh, as though it were still there. The midday sun made it burn still more. The heat did not dissipate but moved deeper into his body, creating an unquench-able thirst. Baz's parched throat began to ache. He focused on the knots, but every so often he felt the little dog rub up against his leg, its heart beating steadily like a clock, reminding Baz that his work was being timed.

* * *

Baz puffed up the mound of hay before sinking into it, trying to convince himself of its softness. But he knew better. Each night it got flatter and finer, and Baz grew more accustomed to the hardness of the stable floor.

Baz looked at the shape of Dagar's thin out-stretched body, at the spaces unfilled by hay or flesh. He reached for some hay from another mound and poked it into the emptiness.

"The master doesn't like you moving the hay," said Dagar. "You'll find yourself sleeping on the bare floor."

"It doesn't matter," said Baz, returning to his place.

At first Baz would fall asleep at once, too tired to dream. And he would awake with the feeling that no time had passed at all, that there were no nuances between night and day. But then he began to dream, the past and present swirling into a colorful tapestry of people and places. One night he saw himself floating above the fields of madder on a flying carpet, drifting further and further from his present life. When he awoke he turned to Dagar.

"Have you ever tried to leave?" he asked.

"You mean escape?" said Dagar, his eyes widening with fear. "The ones who have tried are brought back and punished. Then I don't know if they are taken away or die. Besides, there is no way to escape."

The master kept the gate locked and he never took his eyes off them during the day. Still, the more

Baz dreamed, the more it seemed possible. His designs, which at first had been simple, reflecting the patterns of his life, became bold and daring.

"We could go to another village and find work there," said Baz.

"And if the master found us?" said Dagar.

"The world is big," said Baz, not knowing if he spoke the truth but wanting to believe it.

4

WHEN LUNCH WAS FINISHED THE BOYS dropped their dishes in the bowl of muddy water and returned to their weaving.

The master made his rounds, stopping behind each of them and striking his whip against the ground. When he came to Dagar he struck the boy's back and the rolled tapestry fell to the ground.

"What have we here?" said the master, leaning

over to pick it up. He unrolled it and spread the tapestry across his thigh.

"Ahh," said the master, shaking his head. "How lovely."

"That's mine," said Dagar, stretching his hand forward.

"Where did you get it?" demanded the master.

"It was a gift," said Dagar. "From my former master."

"Well then," said the master. "I bought you and all of this." He cracked the whip against the dry earth, sending the dust into fits. "So I believe it is mine."

Dagar grabbed the tapestry and would not let go. The master snapped the whip and Dagar ducked to avoid its sting. But he fell to the ground, taking the master with him. They scrambled in the dirt flecked with scraps of rubbish and tiny shards of broken ceramic. A key surfaced from the rubble, and like a bird of prey, Baz crouched down, swept it up, and dropped it into his pocket.

The master clambered to his feet and sent the whip flying again. "That is mine," he said, striking Dagar's hand. He poised the whip above Dagar's head, ready to thrash again.

Dagar dropped the tapestry and stepped back, his hand bleeding.

"Back to work," cried the master.

Reluctantly, Baz returned to weaving. Although the master had not struck him, he thought he could feel the sting of the whip against his own hands. And he felt the sorrow of his friend, who had lost a dear possession. Last, he felt the weight of the key in his pocket. He knew not what it opened, only that it represented a way out.

The remainder of the day stretched out longer than usual, as though someone had lengthened the hours across a loom.

Dinner came and went. There was no mention of the tapestry or the key. Baz and Dagar lay down on their mounds of hay to sleep. When the master came to bid them good night he deposited a loose scrap of homely fabric at Dagar's feet.

"Consider it a fair trade," he said.

When the master had left, Baz took the key from his pocket. He had not dared to look at it until now. But it was dark and he could only feel its outline against his fingers, a long stem with three loops at the end.

"Look what I found," he said. "Maybe it opens the gate."

"I don't think so," said Dagar.

"We must try," said Baz.

"Another whipping and I may break in two," said Dagar. He rolled the scrap of homely fabric and tucked it under his tunic.

Baz lay awake waiting until the sounds had worn themselves out from exhaustion. Then he roused Dagar and they took their few belongings and left the stable. The master was sleeping in an outbuilding nearby. His snores rippled the night air as they passed. When they got to the gate Baz took a last look around. He squeezed the key in his fist, then fit it into the lock. But it would not turn.

"It is not the right key," sighed Dagar.

Baz tried the key again but it still wouldn't turn.

They returned to the stable. In the morning it seemed that they'd woken from another dream. Baz reached in his pocket for the key and held it up to the sun shining in through a crack in the ceiling. It was as beautiful as Baz's tapestry, the tip carved in an intricate pattern of designs.

"I will offer to give this to the master in return for the tapestry," said Baz.

"He will take both," said Dagar. "You'd best keep it for as long as you can. Perhaps it is worth something."

Baz dared not put the key in his box among his things or guard it on his person. So he dug into the mound of hay and buried it.

The sun had just begun to set, floating downward, dipping behind the far-off mountains. The master had filled their tin cups with water. Baz sipped slowly, savoring each drop, willing it to expand. Dagar was crouched down next to the little dog, Blink, who had become a regular visitor since Baz's arrival.

"He likes you," said Dagar. The dog was licking the rim of the boy's cup, lapping up the few remaining drops clinging to the edges.

"Maybe you'd better save some for yourself," said Baz.

"I'm not thirsty," said Dagar. He stood up and returned to his weaving. But he worked more slowly than usual. His breathing was shallow and beads of sweat had begun to form along his hairline.

"You're sick," said Baz.

Dagar did not answer but stepped back from his work into a corner. He retched, but all his empty stomach gave up was a green liquid bile that Blink circled sniffing, then lapped up. The sight made Baz feel queasy and he worried that he, too, might be falling ill. But it was only disgust.

"Ohh," cried the master, wielding his whip and striking Dagar across the back. "Sickness is not permitted here."

Dagar dropped to the ground. Blink trotted over to him and licked the boy's hands, curled in tight fists. But the master whipped the dog as well. Then he lifted Dagar over his shoulder and carried him away. Dagar did not return for dinner, nor did he return to the stable to sleep.

A day passed, then two more. Each morning Blink trotted into the courtyard as Baz began to weave. He sat back on his haunches in Dagar's empty space and started to whine. Occasionally, he would roam around the other boys working, but then he would return to Dagar's place and begin to whimper.

"What's all this cacophony?" shouted the master. He glared at Blink, who began to yelp loudly. Suddenly, the master lashed out at the dog with his whip.

Blink sprang to his feet, but the master continued to thrash the little dog until he collapsed, writhing in pain.

"Stop," cried Baz.

Paying no heed, the master took a broom and swept Blink aside just as he did the threads that rained to the ground during the workday.

"Let that be a reminder," he said. "Of how I reward ingratitude."

"Where is Dagar?" asked Baz.

The master raised his eyebrows and shrugged. He didn't answer. But when the sun set, its final ribbons of light crossing the sky like loosely woven threads, Baz knew that Dagar would not return.

❋ ❋ ❋

Baz collapsed into sleep, exhausted, the day's happenings whirring in his brain. He slept fitfully, waking to darkness and a low moaning in the distance. It was Blink. Baz stared into the darkness until his eyes could make out the shape of Dagar's empty bed of hay. The little dog's whimpering stopped, but then started again, louder than ever.

Baz got up quietly and went outside. The moon was nearly full, illuminating the courtyard in broken shards of white light. Blink lay in a corner, kicked, beaten, and broken in places.

So this is death, thought Baz, feeling powerless. He couldn't bear to watch the animal suffer. He stood perfectly still, letting the moonlight reveal himself, the dog, the truth of the stranger who had sold him into labor with a cruel master, and the truth of what he was about to do.

The master's booth was locked, but one of the windows was broken. It was easy for Baz to stretch his arm through the empty space. The tips of his fingers were just long enough to grasp the handle of the cabinet drawer. Baz pulled it open. Inside were snippets of carpet, colored squares with designs from which to work. Beneath them lay the gun.

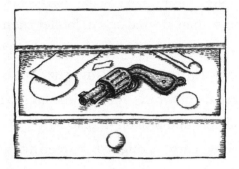

Baz had never held a gun, and the metal felt cold and unfamiliar. He didn't know if it was loaded or not. But he was willing to leave that to fate.

He moved quietly across the courtyard to where Blink lay, his eyes closed. Baz didn't try to escape from the rays of light that shone down onto him, illuminating his deed. He wrapped a corner of his tunic around the weapon to muffle its sound. He pulled the trigger and the gun went off. Blink's body jerked briefly, then twitched to a stop. The breathing ceased and he was free.

Baz wrapped Blink's body in a scrap of discarded fabric from a mound of uncollected garbage outside the booth. He wished to bury the animal, but he had no tools. So he carried the dog to the garden and began to dig a hole with his hands between the rows of summer flowers, their heads bent, buds locked tight. The dirt was dry and light and moved easily. Baz finished quickly. Then he laid Blink in the open grave, covering it with earth, weeds, and fallen petals.

"Goodbye, Blink," he said.

Baz returned the gun to the drawer and went back to the stable. He lay down in the hay, his body curled in a tight ball. He was shivering, chilled by the force of his own deed. In that moment fear and cold merged, a single emotion that rose to the surface of his body and ruled. The little dog's whimpering, though but a memory, continued to sound in the back of his mind, nearly as real as before.

"Forgive me, Blink," Baz whispered. He dared not close his eyes, but fixed them on a spot on the wall where they rested until dawn. He reached beneath him into the layers of hay until he could feel the key, which continued to fill him with endless possibilities, opening doors to escape and freedom.

"Oh where, oh where has my little dog gone?" The master was singing, circling the bloody ground with his whip. He stopped and spit, then planted himself behind Baz. The fear and cold Baz had felt the night before had turned into a searing heat that moved in waves through his chest and rose to his temples.

Baz willed his attention toward his weaving. Deep fiery reds spiraled through the threads like balls of energy waiting to be released.

Baz waited for the master to leave, but he stood firm, blocking Baz's light, forcing him to squint, and breathing down his neck.

At lunchtime Baz was given an extra plate of food.

"A deed such as that needs to be rewarded," said the master. "If I'd known you were so eager, I would have asked you to do it."

Baz knew he was referring to Blink.

"You've spared me that distasteful task," the master said, rubbing the lobe of his ear between his thumb and forefinger. "Perhaps your ability could be put to better use elsewhere. Though it would be a shame to lose you," he added. "You show such promise."

The master began to drum his fingertips on the table. When the boys got up to leave, he stopped Baz.

"You come with me," he said, leading Baz to his booth and sitting him down on the stool. The master reached into the drawer and took out a piece of felt. "Yesterday you were soft, like this," he said, placing the felt in Baz's left hand. Then he reached for the gun. "Now you've become hard," he said. "Like this." He dropped the gun in Baz's right hand. "It's time to move on. Tomorrow you will come with me."

The master took back the felt and squeezed it in his palm. Then he took the gun. "I'll have to find another home for this," he said wistfully.

❀ ❀ ❀

Baz felt the whip, limp now, crawl up the back of his leg.

"Rise and shine," said the master. He had

prepared a large breakfast for them both. There were eggs, fruit, bread, and a sweet syrupy tea.

"Where are we going?" asked Baz when they'd finished eating.

"To the marketplace," said the master. "It is easy to find boys with nimble fingers. But boys like you fetch a pretty price. Get your things. The captain is waiting. He's looking for boys like you."

"What do you mean?" asked Baz. "Am I to become a soldier?"

"Killing a dog and killing a man. Taking a life. Is it not the same?" The master chuckled to himself.

Baz now knew his fate. He would be sold as a mercenary and taken to fight in some strange land of tribal battles, something he knew nothing about. He had heard of that happening to others, but never imagined that it could happen to him.

The other boys had risen and were washing in the trough of dirty water. They looked wide-eyed at Baz as he entered to collect his belongings. He emptied his few possessions into his satchel, then reached beneath the layers of hay for the key. Dagar's voice came to him, like grains of pollen carried by the wind. "Keep it for as long as you can. Perhaps it is worth something."

"Goodbye," he said to the others, turning his back on them and their gaze, which followed him to the courtyard, where the master waited with his horse.

"Get on," he ordered. Baz climbed up onto the back of the horse just as he had done not long before. He glanced around him, unable to focus on the objects surrounding him. All earthly ties, all feeling, was wound into a tight spool in the center of his heart. In his mind he was still weaving fiery reds and oranges into bold patterns and cryptic designs. He thought that somewhere in this trauma must be the meaning of life, which seemed to no longer make any sense.

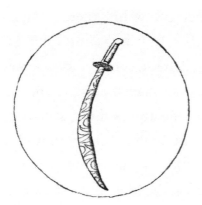

5

TADIS WALKED ALONG WITH NO SHOES. HIS feet felt the dry ground, tracing the contours of the earth beneath. For days, he'd felt the rumbling below, sensed the energy ripple upward and outward. Sometimes he would let himself go with the motion and he would lose his balance. He knew what the earth was telling him, what the rumbling meant. He would not be able to stop it. It was written in the destiny of a people and he was part of it. He continued walking, his light gray tunic, which reached below his knees, swaying rhythmically with his gait. It was simply cut, but its weave was decorated with symbols of a long-lost script. Tadis's head was shaved close to the scalp. He carried a sword beneath his tunic, strapped to his body by a belt. Sometimes when he moved, the sides of the tunic would part, giving way to a vision of the sword's jeweled handle. Behind him he pulled a two-wheeled cart that opened to a table when he performed. In the cart were the props of his trade. He was a magician.

It was dusk and the curtain of descending darkness sharpened his senses. He registered the sounds of the coming night, the silence. Then he moved his mind beyond what was before him, until it seemed he was walking in a dream. In the dream there was a boy in a market square. He was moving toward that boy. Tadis knew the dream to be true. He stopped and spread a rough woolen blanket on the ground. Lying down, he closed his eyes, but reminded himself to rise with the sun because the boy, though he didn't know it, would be waiting for him. Beneath his body, he could still hear the distant rumbling.

* * *

Baz stood at the edge of the marketplace. It was unbearably hot and the heat from the ground below rose to meet the air above in an invisible belt of oppression. The master tied his horse to a post and nudged Baz into the throng of people coming to sell their wares. There were terra-cotta pots piled high, and lengths of colored fabric, woven carpets, dried fruit, and spices, a feast for the eyes. At the far end of the square a group of young boys were gathered. Soldiers passed from one to the next betting on who would make a good warrior.

Baz looked at the soldiers, wondering how they, with the same seeds, same flesh, same blood, could be so different from him. He knew that life had forged them into this circumstance. Their destiny had been shaped in the same way his father molded wooden figures with his knife, not knowing why.

A soldier stopped before Baz, and the master pulled him aside and began to speak, his voice low but his body animated by movement. The soldier's eyes settled on Baz with interest. Baz turned away, not wanting to witness his own sale. But then the master's attention was caught by the edge of a sword glittering in the sunlight. Riveted, spellbound, he forgot the figure before him, forgot even about Baz, and turned to the bearer of the sword. His head was shaved close to his scalp and his cheekbones were set high in his face, telling Baz that he was not from these parts. Another stranger, he thought.

"How much do you want for your sword?" asked the master.

The man pointed his sword to the east. The sun was climbing higher in a sky that had faded to the color of ash. Then he swung it in a circle and returned it to the belt strapped around his waist. "My sword is not for sale," he said.

"Ohh," crooned the master, grinning widely. "Perhaps I can convince you." He reached into the worn leather pouch that bulged from his waist and extracted a fistful of gold pieces. A teasing breeze interrupted this exchange, winding its way through the market-place, setting the canvas awnings flapping. The skirt of the man's tunic flew open, revealing the long metal sheath of the sword. Baz stood back, his spine tingling.

"I don't want your money," said the man. Then he turned to Baz. "However, I will take the boy."

The master's eyes, small, dark bullets, darted from the sword to Baz, then back again to the man before him.

"Sold," he said. He cast a feverish look at Baz. "My lucky charm. Go, now." He smiled, his gold tooth capturing the sun's rays, sending them back to their source. The master took the sword from the man and caressed it, moving his palm up the blade to the very tip. Then he turned the treasure in his hand, pivoting the blade earthward. A small door in the handle slid open to reveal an empty compartment. The master, his eyes fixed on the blade, did not notice.

"So now you are mine," said the man, his eyes narrowing to small slits so that Baz could not read their expression. Baz flinched at the idea of ownership being applied to his person.

The man before him did not have a horse like the other soldiers, just a small closed box on wheels, which he pulled behind him. "Are you coming?" he asked.

It was a question, not a command, and Baz, barely realizing it, turned to follow the fine trail etched by the cart's wheels.

The man walked erect, his eyes facing forward. Baz's mind raced ahead. There was nothing stopping him from bolting. He had no idea where home was, but he knew deep inside that if he could trust and give himself up to it, he would be taken there. Baz took a deep breath, about to act on his thought, when the man turned to face him.

"You are in the future," he said. "But the present is where things happen."

"What are you talking about?" said Baz angrily, annoyed that the man seemed to have read his mind, angry that he'd lost his chance.

"You do not have to come with me," said the man.

"But you bought me," said Baz.

"And now I'm giving you the choice to join me or to go." Seconds ago that choice would have seemed easy, but now that it was put before him like this, Baz hesitated. And in those seconds of doubt, the earth began to rattle. His memory stirred. It was the same rumbling that Baz had heard with Melesh and the stranger in the stable. It seemed ages ago. Only this time the rumbling didn't cease. It grew louder and louder until in the distance the earth yawned open, cracking like large sheets of terra-cotta. The ground slid from under Baz's feet, causing him to lose his balance. He heard cries from the market-place, saw colors moving in spirals. Then he felt the weight of earth falling around him, dirt in his mouth, grainy and sharp.

Baz lay very still, afraid to stir. He could still hear the rumbling, feel the ground vibrating beneath his limbs. He'd thought of many ways of dying, but he had never thought of being buried before he was even dead.

"You will not die," said the man. He was crouched low to the ground, leaning over Baz, who had forgotten the presence of his keeper. The man took a drink of water from a small gourd, then offered it to Baz. "This may be scarce, so we must use it sparingly."

He helped Baz to his feet. "You have never experienced an earthquake?" he said. "Why, this was just a minor one."

To Baz it looked as if the world had tipped over onto its side, spilling its contents over the surface. He had felt rumblings of the earth but had never seen it heave and retch like this, spitting things from its center, swallowing objects. Baz looked in the direction from which they'd come. Once, there had been one road leading from the village, sunken into the earth, paved by years of travel, hard dirt pushed together by sheer force. But there was no road now. It had been torn asunder and strewn in many directions, covered in rubble. Baz felt small and insignificant in front of the earth's vengeance.

"There is no longer a road," he whispered, struck not so much by its absence as by the impression that there was no returning, no following the path back to his previous life.

Baz glanced at the objects that had been flung far and wide, now lying randomly about. They reminded him of all he'd been separated from, filling him with longing for his old life with its solid props of familiarity and affection. He picked up a tin box, like the one in which his mother stored sweets and sugared ginger.

What will happen to this? he thought. In his other hand was a ceramic plate smeared with soil and chipped along its edge. He longed to return these objects to their owners, but knowing that wasn't possible he placed them upright, trying to restore some of their dignity. The man who had bought him was beside him righting his cart. Although it had fallen to one side, it had not turned over and nothing had spilled out.

"I guess you're lucky," said Baz.

"I guess I am," said the man, forcing a smile. "I guess these things are meant to stay with me for the time being."

"Where are we going?" asked Baz, who had lost all desire to bolt. The man had been right and this was the proof. It was useless to look toward the past. He had nothing but the present. Besides, he wanted to know what was in the cart.

"We will travel toward the west," said the man, who had already set himself in motion, measuring his steps cautiously upon the crooked earth. "We are still far from our destination."

Baz wondered if he might not have been better off

buried by the earth than following this man toward the unknown. But it was only for a moment. The way in which the earth had settled had somehow changed the way he looked at his own life. He borrowed the reasoning of the man before him. Apparently, he was not meant to be a weaver. And perhaps he wasn't meant to be with this man either. But he would have to figure that out for himself.

Baz put one foot in front of the other because that was all he could do. He caught up to the cart and then to the man who walked before him.

"I am called Tadis," said the man. "What is your name? You do have a name."

"I do," said Baz, irritated at this person who seemed to think he knew everything. "But there are people with no names. I once met a man who had no name."

Tadis's eyebrows arched upward. He looked at Baz curiously.

"But he had a horse," said Baz. "He was fond of that horse."

"So he became the Man Who Loved His Horse," said Tadis.

"How did you know?" asked Baz.

"Well, what else?" said Tadis, chuckling to himself.

6

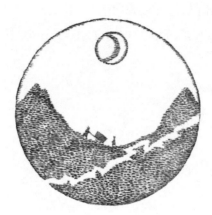

IN THE DAYS THAT FOLLOWED THEY CAME across people fleeing with their possessions. A man came from the desert, his face wrapped in a scarf.

"Were many homes destroyed?" he asked. "Did many people die?"

"I don't think so," said Tadis. "They are fleeing from fear. Fear of another earthquake. They are fleeing from the future. And that will take them to but one place."

By now Baz knew the answer to that. "The present," he said.

"Yes," said Tadis. "And only then will they reclaim their lives again." He picked up a child's drum and handed it to a small boy running back and forth in a small puddle welled up from the earth. His eyes were large with wonder but he was too young to judge the earth's action. It was not the same for Baz, who felt himself ever more tightly wrapped in a web of betrayal. His body grew rigid as he thought how first he'd been betrayed by the man with the horse, then by the master. Now he'd been betrayed by the very earth upon which he walked.

"The earth must move, too," said Tadis, sensing Baz's despair. "When it becomes too intense in places, it shifts. That is the law of energy. It is always seeking a balance."

In a distant town a bell chimed. Baz stopped to listen and to wonder at its meaning.

"Now it will be a reminder of what has happened," he said. The event has given it meaning, thought Baz, puzzling at this backward way of looking at the world, at how people attached meaning randomly. Had the earth made him see this?

"Come," said Tadis, urging Baz on. "We have a long journey."

"What is in your cart?" asked Baz, feeling brave.

"That is where I keep my tricks," said Tadis.

Baz was puzzled. "Tricks?" he said.

"Warriors must know many tricks," said Tadis. "How else would they outsmart their enemies?"

"Of course," said Baz absently. He was thinking no longer of the present but of the sleepy little town that had been his home. How often he had awoken wishing, waiting for something to happen. Now he chided himself. He had gotten what he wished for.

"I'll bet you don't have a trick to change what has happened," he said to Tadis.

"The earthquake, you mean? No, I cannot change what has happened. I cannot change the course of a river as long as I'm swimming against it. I must go with the river. I must become one with the river. Then, yes, I can change something."

That seemed silly to Baz. "How does one become one with the river?" he asked impatiently. He felt tired and was not in the mood for this man's philosophical musings.

The cart began to squeak as if it had something to say.

Tadis spoke. "It's not in the mind," he said. "It's here. He placed his broad palm on the center of his chest. "In the heart."

Baz still didn't understand, so he dropped it. "Weren't you sorry to part with your sword?" he asked. "Don't you need it?"

"You were not bought for money," said Tadis. "You were bought for something far more valuable: that man's desire to have the sword, to possess."

"But you must have wanted me more than that sword," said Baz, realizing just how much the world turned on people's desires. How desire drove people to hate and to love. Desire for money, for riches, for power, for pleasure. The list was endless. "So your desire becomes my destiny. That's not really fair, is it?"

"Your destiny is not what you think," said Tadis.

"I am now to become a mercenary because that's what was wished of me," said Baz.

"By whom?" said Tadis.

"By the master. By everyone but me," said Baz. He sighed. "So I will become a warrior."

"Someday," said Tadis. "But not in the way that you think."

Baz had never thought of desire as a tool for barter. He'd never really thought of desire at all. He had wished for things in life, but never so desperately as to call it desire. But in the coming days when he was thirsty, hungry, homesick, or tired, he was able to study desire in all of its complexity. That strange sensation that magnified his senses, the painful want of something beyond his reach.

Darkness came, a welcome return to order in a day fraught with chaos. Tadis did not stop, preferring to travel by night and rest by day.

"Do we walk in darkness not to be seen?" asked Baz. His eyes had not yet grown accustomed to the shadows.

"No," said Tadis. "We walk in the dark to learn to see."

That made no sense to Baz, no more than much

else of what Tadis said. But he was too tired to argue. So he followed willingly, gladly engulfing himself in the coolness of night.

Tadis continued. "Darkness is a cloak that allows us to believe we are not seen," he said. "But in darkness our physical boundaries are removed, in the same way we remove the limitations of our minds. That's what allows us to see. What we see in darkness can be more real than what we see in light. In light we put up the boundaries again and things that seemed possible in the dark no longer seem so. That is a trick that our minds play on us."

"Everyone plays tricks with their minds," said Baz. He had been playing one of his own, imagining that each step he took would take him closer to home.

"There are more tricks in our minds than I could ever fit in this little cart of mine," said Tadis.

Baz wished to see just what was in the cart, but there was no point looking now in the dark. Tomorrow he would ask.

"Listen," said Tadis.

Baz found himself listening without really wishing to. He heard the sound of his own breath and that of Tadis. He heard the sound of his own footsteps. He noticed that when he couldn't see, his hearing became more acute, his sense of touch finer. He was sure that he could even taste the night air, and the heat that had remained trapped in its molecules. As Baz walked on, his eyes grew accustomed to the dark and he could make out the form of Tadis and his cart moving steadily ahead. They had distanced themselves from the area of the earthquake and Baz could now see the dim outline of the road they traveled, and the silhouettes of the spare trees that seemed to sprout randomly with a purpose he could not know.

Baz pinched himself to stay awake. The darkness, which at first had seemed large and foreboding, had dwindled into a black satin curtain of softness in which he wished only to lie down and sleep.

* * *

As the sun appeared on the horizon they were approached by a woman traveling alone. She was looking for her son, who had been at the marketplace on the day of the earthquake. She walked up to Baz and took him by the shoulders.

"You are my son," she said. Though he knew this was not so, Baz saw in the woman's tearstained face that of his own mother. And he had to fight back tears.

"I'm sorry, but you've made a mistake," he said. Here was desire again parading as truth. The woman wanted so badly to find her son that she allowed herself to be fooled.

The woman began to shake Baz as though doing so might turn him into something he was not. Then she fell to the ground and began to beat the earth with her fists. Dust rose, but the earth wouldn't budge any more than her son would appear. Tadis bent over the woman. He touched her shoulders and spoke gently. The woman, calmed, clutched his arms, then stood up and continued on her way. Baz followed her with his gaze, haunted by how she resembled his own mother. For a moment he fought the urge to run after her.

Tadis began to look for a spot to rest in a field off the road, rife with wild grain and yellow flower buds that reminded Baz of home. Tadis flattened the grain until it made a cushion beneath them. Then he took a wool blanket from his cart and laid it over the grain. Baz fell to the ground and stretched his body across the earth. He felt the layer of coolness that had sunk in during the night and hugged his body. Above him the heat was descending. He had never slept during the day and he thought he would not be able to close his eyes because of the light. Under his tunic, deep in his pocket, he felt the key press into his body.

Beside Baz sat Tadis, his hands opened skyward,

whispering something that Baz could not make out. Then Tadis lay down on his back, his face pointing upward. The bones of his skull, prominent in places, reminded Baz of the plates of the earth. And he sadly remembered the little dog, Blink. His bones had been visible like that, too. Baz sighed. He noticed thankfully that his weary body paid no heed to the light. His thoughts quieted, too, until they were mere whispers unable to rouse him from deep slumber.

They slept until dusk, when they rose and began their travels again. This time the desire for rest had been replaced by hunger. They journeyed through the night, Baz wondering all the while where they were going. As the sun rose, they entered a village. News of the earthquake had arrived and people spoke of nothing else. But news traveled slowly, and it had been transformed much like a river that twisted and bent its course so that when it reached its destination it had changed so much that it was not the same river that left its source.

People talked of the earth turning inside out, and Baz hazarded a guess as to what that meant.

"It has a different meaning for each of us," said Tadis. "Someday you will know what the meaning has been for you."

They wandered through the market stalls, mixing with the throngs of animated people chatting and exchanging wares. They passed the vendors of colorful carpets, and images of Dagar and little Blink came back to Baz in a tightly knit pattern of color and movement.

Baz looked longingly at the trays of nuts and the baskets of fruit, their colors vibrating in the light. He waited in vain for Tadis to buy or bargain for some food.

"I have no money," said Tadis, shrugging. "Remember I purchased you with a sword."

"But you must have something in your cart you

can trade for some food," said Baz, unable to bear the hunger that made his stomach contract in little waves.

"Warriors do not always have the occasion to eat," said Tadis.

Baz fixed his eyes for a moment on a stack of flatbread, his mouth watering. He was rummaging in his pockets for something he might offer in exchange. Suddenly his desire to hang on to the key weakened in the face of his growing hunger, and he was about to offer it to a vendor. But a crowd had gathered around Tadis, who had opened his cart and was now giving a show, moving balls from under cups faster than the eyes could see. Then he gathered the balls and began to juggle, adding another, then another, which seemed to appear from nowhere. The audience cried out in wonder, dropping coins at Tadis's feet.

Tadis emptied the pockets of his tunic, turning them inside out. Then he waved a red handkerchief

through the air and tied the corners, making a small
sack. When he opened the sack, it was filled with
fruit, nuts, and flatbread. The audience applauded
again while Tadis folded the handkerchief back up,
then waved it before the crowd, empty. He reached
into his pocket and pulled out another satchel filled
with the fruit, nuts, and flatbread.

"So you are a magician after all," said Baz when
the act was finished. His hunger seemed to be running the gamut of his emotions, trying on each for
size. It was now clothed in grumpiness. "You trick
people into believing what isn't true."

"How can you know what is true?" said Tadis. "Truth is a journey that you have not yet begun. People believe what they want to believe. You saw that in the woman who thought you were her son. But yes, you are right. I am a magician of sorts." Tadis smiled at Baz and opened the cloth bag strapped to his waist. "You see? I have come up with something for us to eat." Tadis swung the satchel from side to side, then sat down under a tree in the village square, offering its contents to Baz first, then helping himself.

Baz bit into the bread eagerly, letting its texture play against his tongue and the sides of his cheeks. Nothing had ever tasted that good. He gazed at the sun, which was climbing higher into the sky. Far off in the distance the mountains loomed large.

"Is that where we're going?" asked Baz.

Tadis followed Baz's gaze. "To the top of the mountain," he said.

"They seem so close," said Baz.

Tadis nodded. "But that is an illusion. As we move closer, it will seem that they, too, move, farther into the distance. And then the water, and the desert will appear, and the forest, and all things in between. It is as though the mountains are tricking us."

"The mountains cannot trick us," said Baz. "They are inanimate."

"The mountains have a soul," said Tadis. "Like all of nature. It is what links them to us in the big tapestry of life where we are all one."

Baz had heard stories about the mountains, but he had never heard that they had a soul. "They say that many people have died trying to reach the top," he said. His eyes narrowed and he felt the muscles of his body tighten at the thought.

"Perhaps that is so," said Tadis. He picked up a leaf, dry and wrinkled, and he blew it into the air, watching it catch on a passing current. "This leaf has a soul, too. And it resonates with yours. That is, if you choose for it to."

This was the second time that Tadis had mentioned choice.

"Choice?" said Baz. "I thought I was nothing but a servant. And a servant does what he is told."

"I have no wish to tell you what to do," said Tadis. "That would be too easy for both of us. It is you who must decide."

Baz was silent. He felt stillness settle around him. "Are you saying I am free?"

"Of course," said Tadis. "If that is what you choose."

"What will it cost me?" said Baz, frowning. He still did not fully trust the man before him.

"I cannot say. That, too, is for you to decide," said Tadis.

Baz's thoughts darted to and fro like the leaf blowing through the air. He fixed his gaze on a spot on the ground to stop them. In its center a tiny chip of mica sparkled like a miniature sun giving off rays of light. It reminded Baz of the sword with its jeweled handle, and of the stranger's message. "You will follow the light."

Baz sighed. "If this is my destiny I must follow it," he said.

"Then you wish to continue?" said Tadis getting to his feet.

"Yes," said Baz. "I will continue."

"But first we must rest," said Tadis.

7

THEY LEFT THE MARKETPLACE, TURNING DOWN a narrow street of the village. They hadn't gone far when they were stopped by a boy who was not much younger than Baz. He had seen the magician's tricks.

"I had nothing to pay you with, but I can give you a room to rest," he said, lowering his eyes. "Follow me."

The boy led them to a row of squat houses. In

the last was a series of interlocked rooms flanked by a large eating area with two rectangular tables of wood. The boy poured tea for them, and offered them plates of pulses and dried fruit.

"Each day I watch travelers come and go and I long to follow them," he said, sighing.

"Once I felt just like you," said Baz. "But now I'm not so sure."

"I traded my sword for you," said Tadis. "And my act for this meal and a bed. Perhaps you two can trade places."

"Sometimes I long for my old life," said Baz. "Where nothing happened."

"Something was always happening," said Tadis. "Otherwise you wouldn't be here. This young man thinks nothing is happening. But if he looks back five days from now, fairly, he will see that much has happened."

"Maybe," said the boy. "But they won't be big happenings." He sounded disappointed.

"That depends on how you choose to view them," said Tadis. He took an egg from the boy's basket. "This seems small."

"The hen lays eggs every few days at this time of year," said the boy.

"And that is a big event," said Tadis, "if you look at it for what it is." He stirred a cube of dark sugar into his tea and watched the crystals dissolve into the hot liquid, all becoming one. The two boys looked at each other, not quite knowing what to make of the man before them.

Baz drank his tea and bit into a fig, letting the seeds roll across his tongue and catch in his teeth. The sweetness made his mouth water. He had been hungry for so long that he could now taste the fig to its fullest. "This is the best fig I've ever had," he said, causing Tadis to smile.

After they'd eaten, the boy led them to a room with two mattresses covered in cotton, spread across the floor, bleached bright by the sun. Next to the room was a small closet with a bowl of water for washing and soap that smelled of the flower petals from Baz's home.

How the scents of my life follow me, thought Baz. He knew that if he were smelling the soap for the first time now, it would be stamped with the memory of this place. But instead the smell was of home, where he'd first sampled it.

Baz lay down on the cotton sheet, which felt cool. He was surprised at how quickly his body adapted to sleeping by day and traveling by night. His muscles and bones gave in to the softness of the mattress, which felt very different from the ground. Tadis lay next to him. Baz noticed that he prayed before sleep, but he didn't listen to the man's words. He felt it was rude. Baz quietly said his own prayers, recalling each of his family and his precious friends. He felt that when he prayed he was speaking to them, and he always wondered if they could hear him.

Baz noticed Tadis watching him and he lowered his head shyly. "I don't know if they can really hear me," he said.

"That depends on you," said Tadis. "And your intention."

"Intention?" said Baz. "You mean in my mind I must think that they're listening." How many times had he heard this? The old shepherd back home was always saying something of the same sort.

"No," said Tadis. "Intention does not come from the mind, though the mind thinks it does. Intention comes from here." Tadis pointed to his heart again, then closed his hands in prayer.

Baz closed his eyes and imagined his heart. It was filled with feeling—longing, sadness, each connected to some past event. Anger was there, too, clear and strong, a force that kept him moving. When he focused on it, his body began to feel hot, his earlobes reddened. In one tiny pocket there was joy. He could glimpse it but was not sure how to retrieve it, and he was too tired to ask, or to make the effort. So he said instead, "Where do you come from?"

"Where we come from is not important," said Tadis. "It is where we are going that matters."

"Please don't talk in riddles," said Baz. "I am too tired for that."

"All right," said Tadis. He began. "I was trained to be a warrior like my father before me, and his before. From the moment I was born I was prepared to die, and that made it easier. I knew it could happen in an instant and I wasn't afraid, only curious as to

how it might come about. In this I felt lucky because I knew that most people aren't prepared for
death, for falling into nothingness. I joined the army
and I began to dream of piecing together a kingdom
from the land. I dreamed of being a king myself. I
tasted power," said Tadis. "But those were illusions."

Baz found he was listening as much to Tadis's
voice, its vibration, its tone, as to his story. There was
no emotion. Baz thought of his own voice, how often
it was harsh and mean since he'd left home. Tadis's
voice was like filtered drops of gold to his ears.

"Then one day I was separated from my army. I
was alone with nothing but the clothes on my
back. I wandered for days, weeks, maybe months. I
ate when I found food, slept when I could walk no
more. At each village I came to I would ask for news
of my army, but there was none. Then I asked for
directions home, and a stranger told me that if I followed a certain road I would meet with a sign that
would direct me."

"And did you?" asked Baz.

"After three days of traveling the same road I met a woman. She had lost her son."

Baz interrupted Tadis. "Like the woman I met."

"Many mothers lose their sons," said Tadis. "Imagine what it is like. The child whom she has brought into the world with great suffering and joy, who has grown from a mysterious seed into a living being."

Baz reminded himself the next time he prayed to do so with intention. That way maybe his mother could hear him.

Tadis continued. "The woman carried a small sack with scraps of fabric that she'd gathered in her travels, and a needle and some thread. She was sewing the squares of cloth together into blankets. She asked me if I would buy one. I had lost all I had and I had nothing left to give her. I told her I was sorry and she said, 'Just give me your hands.' I was ashamed because my hands were dirty, my nails long and black. But I gave them to her. She took them in hers, rough and chapped, and she held them. And I felt heat move through my arms and my whole body. After she'd let go she gave me a cloth blanket and she wished me well. In the days that followed, the cloth became everything to me. The weather changed, releasing fury, and the rains came, and I stopped wherever I found shelter and wrapped myself in the blanket. Then the energy of the earth drove me toward the mountains, where I fasted until my desire for food passed altogether. Dream and reality wove themselves together like the small piece of fabric that I was holding. I dreamed of women, all the women I'd met in my life, and I desired them. And I dreamed of my mother and she would be standing on a piece of land that I knew well. I would go there but she would be gone. I took a job with a man who worked wood. My work was simple and repetitive. I thought it was ugly and I hated it. But after months, perhaps it was years—I lost track of time—I began to feel the wood. And I knew my soul had moved into it."

"My father is a woodworker," said Baz, interrupting Tadis. "But he is going blind and soon he will no longer be able to carve wood."

"He will not need his eyes," said Tadis. "He thinks so. But when he loses his sight he will not lose the feel of the wood. His soul knows and will continue the work for him. He will feel and not see and his creations will be more beautiful than before."

"I hope that's true," said Baz, not really believing. It didn't make sense to him. A lot of what this man said didn't make sense to him.

Baz closed his eyes. He thought of his family with intention and he had sweet dreams of home.

"It was like I was really there," he told Tadis when he awoke. "But that's impossible, isn't it?"

Tadis shrugged. "Nothing is impossible," he said.

They ate again at the long wooden table, one beside the other, taking warm bread and honey that the boy had laid out for them. When they left it was dusk. Baz looked back at the squat little house.

From a window he caught the young boy's eyes. And in them he saw something of himself.

"It's like the woman we met," he said to Tadis. "In her I saw something of my mother. Now I see in this boy something of myself."

Tadis smiled. "In that you have discovered a great truth. So I can no longer accuse you of not knowing."

❋ ❋ ❋

In the weeks that followed they gradually returned to traveling by day and resting when darkness came—the rhythm that Baz knew best. He had again begun to count the days by sunrises and sunsets. But he'd stopped viewing his life from old ways, realizing how much of it had been lived from habit. Habit created expectation, and when that failed, disappointment set in. This way was harder, taking things as they came, but he began to notice details in his surroundings that otherwise would have escaped him.

Meals were no longer three a day as Baz had been accustomed to. There were times when they ate nothing, and hunger welled up in Baz until it seemed it would overflow. He would begin to feel weak, but then his energy would surge again as they happened upon a new settlement or village.

Each village was different in color, in look, in feel. But, underneath, all had that same buzz of activity that made the world turn. In one village Baz stopped before a street vendor to buy some nuts. He had finished those he had brought with him so long ago that he'd forgotten what they looked like. Now he saw these nuts with a fresh eye, noting their varying sizes and shades, their small defects and bumps. Ordinarily he would have left the odd ones behind; this time he took as many different ones as he could find.

"I'm sure each will taste different," he told

himself. He turned, searching for Tadis, but the man had disappeared. Baz walked on and soon found him in the village square. He'd opened his cart and was performing tricks. A small crowd had gathered and people were clapping, urging him on.

Baz stopped to watch as Tadis waved a simple stick before his eyes. Seconds later it had become a snake. The crowd sighed in amazement. They loved this. Then Tadis began to unfold the cloth blanket that had been given to him by the woman on the road. He opened it, then folded it into an accordion, and from its creases he extracted each of the objects spun into the squares of fabric. There was a leaf, a feather, a bright red radish. The audience dropped coins at Tadis's feet and he picked them up, thanking them. Then he closed the cover of his small cart. The crowd would have liked to see more, but Tadis raised a hand in protest.

"How did you make those objects appear?" asked Baz.

Tadis reached in his pocket for a coin. He held it in his palm, then closed his fist. When he opened it, he was holding a button.

"Where did that come from?" asked Baz.

"Here," said Tadis turning his sleeve inside out. There was a pocket sewn in the fabric.

Baz was disappointed. "So your magic is nothing but deception, then," he said. "And you take money for that." It seemed to him dishonest.

"I do not see it that way," said Tadis. "I am simply showing my audience that not all is as it seems. The world is bigger, its secrets greater. True magic is not just to amuse. It's to bring people closer to the truth, to reality. The magician's task is not to show power, but to dispel illusion. Power is nothing but an illusion. Magic represents the capacity for transformation and change inside all of us. Is that lesson not worth something? I, too, must make a living," he said, laughing.

Baz reached for the nuts that he'd stuffed into

the pocket of his tunic. He hadn't been paying attention. "Oh," he cried. "Someone has stolen my nuts." He looked around for the thief.

"I could conjure up someone to blame," said the magician playfully. "It's easily enough done."

"If I hadn't been watching your tricks, then it wouldn't have happened," said Baz.

"So it's my fault," said Tadis.

"No," said Baz. "I am to blame. I was not careful."

"Remember," said Tadis, laughing again. "Magic is the ability to transform, but it is also the ability to forgive. Especially yourself."

Baz looked around again. The streets were suddenly deserted and dust rose from them, creating a haze. People had withdrawn to the coolness of their houses, retreating to make way for the sun, which was at its apex, the hottest hour of the day. In that way the world worked in a careful give-and-take. Tadis and Baz withdrew as well, this time taking shelter under the eaves of an abandoned dwelling on the edge of town. Tadis opened the cloth blanket and spread it across his legs.

"May I touch it?" asked Baz. He wanted to see if it felt any different from what it was—an ordinary piece of fabric. He thought it would have to.

Tadis handed Baz the blanket. He touched it, feeling the texture, running his hands along the hand-sewn seams.

"Is it magic?" he asked.

"Perhaps," said Tadis. "It changed my life, so I guess it must be." He reached for the gourd that he kept under his tunic. It seemed never to be empty. Tadis took a drink, then offered the vessel to Baz.

"Is that gourd magic, too?" asked Baz. "It's always full."

"Let me show you what's magic," said Tadis. He picked up a simple stick from the ground. Then he took a knife and began carving. In no time at all he had a flute, which he handed to Baz.

"I could never do that," said Baz.

"Of course you could," said Tadis. "You must change the way you think. You must change your beliefs."

"But how can I do that?" asked Baz.

"Change begins as a thought," said Tadis. This time he pointed to his head. "Change begins here."

"Anyone can think anything," said Baz, who wasn't impressed.

"But change is stored here," said Tadis, placing his hand on his heart.

Baz placed one hand on his head and the other on his heart. Suddenly it was his head that was pulsating and his heart that seemed to be thinking. He was confused. "Perhaps I'm just tired," he said.

Baz laid his weary body on the ground. He could feel the coolness rising from the earth, but the soles of his feet felt hot. He closed his eyes and imagined himself covered by the cloth that had been sewn together by the woman Tadis had met. And like magic, in his mind the pieces of his life began to form a pattern, until it seemed to Baz that he, too, had been woven into the squares of cloth and become part of it.

Tadis took the flute and began to play.

"Where did you learn that?" asked Baz.

"I learned from the wind passing through the trees," said Tadis.

8

THE EARTH GREW HOTTER AND HOTTER AS
they continued on their journey. The heat, which
had scorched the soles of Baz's feet, had risen
to envelope his entire body. The trees and flowers, which had been thick and brightly colored,
were now dry and sparse, drawing the moisture
into their centers. Baz could feel their thirst, such
longing and desire amplified under the giant

magnifying glass of the sun. They did not have a magic gourd.

"We must be moving toward the desert," said Baz.

"Yes," said Tadis. He had taken the red hand-kerchief from his cart and wound it around his head against the heat.

Baz had never seen the desert, but in the town he was from he'd seen travelers return looking dark and aged from their travels. Like the mountains, the desert was reputed to have claimed the lives of many, lost among the dunes, swallowed by the sands.

The desert was sewn to the rest of the land, seamlessly, just like the squares of the blanket, and when Baz stepped into it, he could not tell where one piece ended and the other began. But soon he was walking through dunes.

"We will need a camel and a guide," said Tadis, pausing to rest. He spread out the cloth blanket, which seemed to have doubled in size, and sat down, crossing his legs.

"Where will we find a guide?" asked Baz.

"Perhaps one will come along. On a camel if we are lucky," said Tadis.

"Can you make that happen?" asked Baz.

"I can increase the probability. That is the task of a magician. If you wish to acquire something you must put the idea in your head. That is one of the four laws of magic—to will."

"To will?" said Baz.

"To intend," said Tadis. "But to do that, first you must clear your head of its cobwebs. You must give the thought space to expand. You must be silent and still."

Baz crossed his legs as Tadis was doing. He looked toward the west, toward the vast strip of horizon that rose from the desert. He tried to silence his thoughts, but as soon as he'd tamed one another popped into his head.

"It is impossible to stop one's thoughts," said Baz.

"It takes practice and persistence," said Tadis. "But it is not impossible."

Baz continued chasing his thoughts, but he could not banish them. He could catch one and observe it, but always another returned. He tried sitting very still and found that if he calmed his breathing his thoughts would slow down.

He and Tadis sat there until Baz's stomach growled loudly from hunger. He could not silence that.

"The body will always distract us," said Tadis, reaching into his pockets and taking out some nuts.

"Those are mine," cried Baz. "The nuts that were stolen. I recognize them."

"So they are," said Tadis. "And where did they come from?"

His eyes were merry and dancing, and Baz could not resist his laughter.

Tadis handed him the nuts and Baz began to break their shells, which he turned into a fleet of small boats in the sand. Tadis opened his satchel and took out some bread that he'd saved, and some fruits whose juice seemed sweeter than anything Baz had ever tasted.

Every so often Baz looked up, hoping to see the guide, yet still not believing that it was possible to conjure up a person from the desert sands. He watched the desert change faces from yellow to beige to blue to pink, depending on the angle of the sun.

"Which color is the desert really?" he asked.

"It varies depending on the movement of all around it. And your own movement. That is because the desert is no more separate from you and me than the mountains."

"Another illusion," said Baz.

"You are a good apprentice," said Tadis. "All things, no matter what color, form, or state, are one boundless being. And though each aspect of that being is unique, it is nonetheless completely and fully the all."

Baz looked puzzled. "How can you know that?" he asked.

"By not using your head," said Tadis. "You must feel it. It is simple, but we make it difficult."

When the sun left the sky the temperature dropped and a chill set in. Baz shivered, squinting into the distance. From the east he could see a small dark figure moving toward them. His heart jumped in amazement.

"It's the guide," he cried.

Tadis remained silent, waiting until the man came closer. His head was wrapped in an ebony cloth. His eyes, dark and somber, looked longingly at them.

Tadis had built a fire and was brewing tea in a tin cup. He offered some to the stranger, who accepted eagerly.

"You will need a guide if you wish to cross the desert," he said. "You can easily lose yourself in the blowing sand."

"You are kind to offer, but we do not need a guide," said Tadis. He poured the man another cup of tea, but the man declined. Instead he shrugged and turned back in the direction from which he had come. Baz watched his shadow disappear into the distance.

"Why did you send him away?" he asked.

"He is not the guide for us," said Tadis. He finished his tea, then extinguished the embers of the fire, watching until the last fleck burned itself out.

Soon the wind started up, scooping up the fine-grained desert sand in its wake. A coolness descended, merging into darkness and fear until each was indistinguishable from the other.

"So this is what we get for sending away our guide," said Baz.

Tadis reached for Baz and drew him closer. Then he wrapped his blanket around them both. The winds grew harsher, whistling, howling. And the sand danced in spirals across the desert floor, picking up speed. Baz wondered if he was meeting death.

"I never thought death would come this way," he

said. But at least he was not alone. His thoughts now came more swiftly, one upon the other, until he could no longer shut them out.

"Ssh."

Baz wasn't sure if it was the wind speaking or Tadis whispering in his ear.

"Do not be afraid," said the voice.

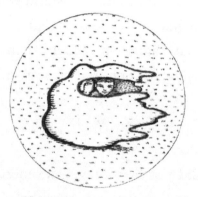

Tadis rose and shifted places, moving them to a sheltered patch of undergrowth.

"Come," he said, pulling Baz to the ground and shielding him with his body.

We shall be buried alive, thought Baz as he felt the sand settle around them, piling up in mounds. In his mind he saw the would-be guide moving away until he was far from reach.

A long time passed. Baz could not quiet his mind, which continued to turn around one thought, that of salvation. Alongside it was love, because he realized that if he were to die he would want to do so with that in his heart. And though he felt anger, even rage, that Tadis had brought them to this, he felt love, too, for the one soul closest to him.

❋ ❋ ❋

The night did not last forever, no more than anything does, and as the sun rose the sand stopped blowing. In the stillness that followed, Baz heard things that he hadn't noticed before. There were the cries of desert animals, and he was sure he could hear the desert flowers unwinding, opening

to greet the sun. When these sounds subsided there was silence. It came not only from outside but from inside, too. His thoughts had stopped, and he was simply happy to be alive.

"We must be going," said Tadis. As they started toward the west an image rose like before, two camels and a solitary wanderer. The wanderer walked behind the camels, and Baz wondered who was leading who.

"That is our guide," said Tadis. They started toward the wanderer and he toward them, as though their paths had been working up to this moment forever. He, like the first man, was bound in dark clothing, and they could make out nothing but his eyes, which were laughing. Even Baz could see that behind them was something very different from the first man they'd met.

Tadis offered the wanderer some gold coins to take them across the desert and the man gladly accepted.

"We must continue," said the guide, not wanting to linger.

They continued until it became too hot to travel. Then the guide stopped. He had a tent to shelter them, which he pitched in the sand. He bade them inside and offered them water and a strange desert fruit with juicy seeds.

"Who are you?" asked Baz.

"I am a wanderer," said the guide, who sat cross-legged, his hands on his knees. "I talk to the desert and it speaks back to me. This is where I belong. I have not seen the world, but it does not matter. I have seen the desert in all of its guises."

"Have you never wished to leave?" asked Baz, thinking of his own longing.

"No," said the guide. "I have met travelers crossing the world, searching. I have heard stories of lands far and near. But in the desert enough happens for an entire lifetime. The desert has given my family and me life, and this is how we give back to it and keep the circle going." The guide swayed in a gentle arc, seemingly unaware of his own motion. "I am part of the desert. The desert is part of me. I could not leave it any more than it could leave me."

Baz had never before thought of himself as being part of anything in that sense, part of a world that he had not created but that had been made long before him. When the earth had separated in the marketplace he had felt separate, severed from his own life and connections. But now he saw that that was nothing but an illusion created by the earth. He, his family, and his life were all part of a greater whole made up of all that was. This was what Tadis called Oneness. Baz was beginning to see it, and feel it.

They continued on, traveling for days. Only

when the sun blinded them or darkness was complete did they stop for a few hours of sleep. As they wandered, the colors surrounding them and everything from the sky to the desert foliage seemed to fade. Baz began to dream of all the brightly painted objects he'd known. And they appeared in his mind without his willing so.

"Look," said Baz. Ahead he saw the image of a small fishing town with boats and pastel houses. But as he approached it, it vanished. Again and again he would see things, only for them to disappear as he got closer. "It's gone before I get there," said Baz.

"Or perhaps it was never there," said Tadis.

This angered Baz. "So now the desert is playing tricks on me," he said.

"Do not be angry," said Tadis. "The desert has the right to create just as you and I do. The right to play tricks, you might say."

One evening they came to a small cluster of

huts. Baz saw them on the horizon and he willed them to stay. To his amazement they did. Baz heard singing and saw birds flying overhead. Children much younger than Baz were playing outside the dwellings. He watched them dart about, stopping to stare as he and Tadis and their guide approached. He could remember a time when he was in their place, marveling at anyone or anything new. He was now the event in their lives, on the other side of the fence. He joined them in a game of rolling balls across the sand. Each ball chose a different path. Sometimes they would meet, then separate again. Baz tried to will his ball to take one road. And when it did he wondered if it was just chance or if that ball had in some way responded to his thought.

In the desert Baz had dreams like never before, and when he entered them he was no longer sure if he was in his head or in another dimension. He dreamed of his brothers.

"If I think of my brothers, will they materialize?" he asked Tadis.

"I do not know," said Tadis. "But you are increasing the probability of it happening."

"Is the mind all that powerful?" said Baz.

"Indeed," said Tadis. "But do not forget that can work both ways. The mind can conjure up beasts and dragons so powerful that they become real."

"I wonder if I will ever see my mother and father again," said Baz aloud.

"That is up to you," said Tadis. "You must put them in your heart as one of your goals."

Baz closed his eyes, intending to imagine his parents in his heart. But when he did this, he was surprised to see that they were already there.

"Do not forget that you have other parents," said Tadis.

"What do you mean?" said Baz.

"You have your father and your mother who brought you into this world. But you have another father and mother, too." Tadis looked skyward. "There is your father." Then he leaned down and sank his hand into the sand. "Your mother springs from the earth. It is she who roots you to the ground."

Baz liked this idea, that wherever he found himself he would have guardians nearby. They weren't related by blood, but they were connected by something even greater, by creation itself. Baz looked at the sky, a deep dark blue, clear and full of stars. They were pulsating, and he could feel them resonate with the beating of his own heart.

"It's as if the stars are trying to tell me something," he said.

"Perhaps they are," said Tadis.

"But how can I know?" asked Baz.

"You must ask," said Tadis.

"I am asking," said Baz. "I have asked many times." He was beginning to feel frustrated.

"Then you are not listening," said Tadis. "Listen, Baz."

As Tadis spoke, Baz felt the heat from his own body expand to envelop him.

"The stars are laughing," Baz said. "Is it possible they are laughing at me?"

"They would never be laughing at you," said Tadis. "But they might be laughing with you."

"They are joyful," said Baz. And despite the earthquake, Dagar, Blink, and all the other losses he'd had, he felt joyful, too.

Tadis looked at the stars, reading them like a road map. "Tomorrow we will leave the desert," he said.

"How did you know the first guide was not for us?" whispered Baz before they slept that night.

"He came from the east," said Tadis. "That is the direction of death and destruction, as any magician knows. The wanderer came from the west. That is the direction of creativity and life."

❋ ❋ ❋

When the random huts on the edge of the desert gave way to a larger village, Tadis spoke. "It is time for us to say goodbye to our guide," he said.

"Where will you go?" Baz asked the guide.

"I will return to the desert," the guide answered. "I will cross back the same way that I came. But all will have changed. I have crossed the desert countless times in my life, and it is never the same."

"One can never go back," said Tadis, laughing. "That's because there is no back. There is only forward. And the only way to go back is to go forward." He looked at Baz. "Have I confused you enough?" he said. And the guide laughed, too.

Baz smiled at this reasoning, which in a funny way had begun to make sense to him. Then Tadis opened his cart and offered the guide something to eat. He had already paid the man, but he gave him a simple carved stick.

"If you are ever lost, this stick will help you find your way," he said, hugging the guide. The guide approached Baz, and Baz noticed for the first time that he had a gold tooth just like the master had. Baz hesitated as the memory of the master's cruelty washed over him. But then he let go of this image and let the guide embrace him. He had not been hugged for a long time, and never by a stranger. But when he joined with this man the strangeness disappeared. Instead, he felt like he'd known him forever.

"Thank you," said Baz.

"It is I who must thank you," said the guide, lowering his head above his hands, which met in a gesture of gratitude.

They watched the guide disappear like a vision on the horizon until his figure was a waning shadow that melted into nothingness.

❋ ❋ ❋

By now Baz had grown accustomed to, even looked forward to, their visits to the villages. Tadis would set up his show in a quiet square and in no time at all people would gather to watch his act. In return for the entertainment, they would give him money, food, or something useful for his travels.

"And now my assistant will juggle for you," said Tadis, opening his cart.

Baz looked at Tadis, startled. He was not prepared for this. He'd practiced juggling many times, but he still hadn't gotten it right. And now Tadis was asking him to perform in front of others. He was doomed to failure.

Baz stepped reluctantly before the crowd.

Tadis handed him five crab apples and he tossed one apple into the air, then another. Pretty soon he'd forgotten that he was being watched, and the apples were spinning round and round in a pretty little circle. Baz was as surprised as his audience, who clapped loudly.

Baz bowed shyly, then stepped back.

"What did you do?" he asked Tadis after the show.

"What did I do?" said Tadis, raising an eyebrow. "Nothing. It's you who performed."

"But I couldn't juggle yesterday without dropping the apples," said Baz.

"That was yesterday," said Tadis. "Today is today."

"Well, I don't see what's changed in my sleep," said Baz.

"No one sees what changes during sleep," said Tadis. "But things do change."

"I didn't have time to think or prepare," said Baz. "What if I'd failed?"

"You didn't fail," said Tadis. "And that's because you didn't have time to think. You just did it. There was no time for your mind to play tricks. Will I or won't I? You outsmarted your mind."

Baz tossed the fruit back to Tadis. Now they were juggling fruit and words.

"I don't understand," said Baz. "Sometimes the mind is important. Then you tell me I must forget all about it."

"You must use your mind, and not let it use you," said Tadis.

The apples were spinning in a lively dance again, and laughter rang out from behind them. They were being watched. In back of them a boy was trying to juggle, forehead wrinkled, eyes squinted as he forced himself to keep them on the crab apples. But each time they fell to the ground, rolling back toward where the boy had been stacking wood. At last he gave up and returned to his task.

"Let me help you," said Baz.

"You don't have to," said the boy.

"But I want to," said Baz. He picked up a block of wood and felt the grain against his skin. Wood reminded him of his father, and he decided that when he touched wood he would in some way be touching his father, because his father and the wood were connected and had been for years. So he liked this work.

"What is your name?" asked Baz.

"Barrel," said the boy.

"I'm Baz."

"Baz the magician," said Barrel.

"I'm not a magician yet," he said. "But maybe someday. Don't worry about not being able to juggle the first time. It's tricky. Why, yesterday I couldn't keep more than three apples in the air."

"Really?" said Barrel.

"Yes," said Baz. "But that was yesterday. Today is today." He smiled as he realized that he'd begun to speak like Tadis.

"Well, maybe I'll be able to juggle tomorrow," said Barrel.

"But it's not worth thinking about until tomorrow comes," said Baz. "Then it will be today."

Barrel looked confused.

"Magicians talk in riddles and rhymes," said Baz. "It's part of what they do." He finished off the stack and then brushed his hands on his tunic.

"I think I can talk in riddles," said Barrel.

"Then I think you can be a magician," said Baz.

A shadow fell over them. A horse had wandered over to the woodpile to rub its coat against the rough blocks. Baz ran his hand along its mane.

"What's your name?" he asked.

"It doesn't have a name," said Barrel.

"I once knew a man without a name, but never a horse," said Baz.

"It has no owner either. It belongs to everyone." Barrel fed the horse a cube of brown sugar that he took from his pocket.

The horse rubbed its head against Baz's shoulder.

"He likes you," said Barrel.

"And I like him," said Baz.

9

THE DAYS PASSED, ONE WOVEN SEAMLESSLY into the next, like the squares in Tadis's blanket.

"We have never stayed long in a village," said Baz to Tadis. "So why are we now?"

"So that we may rest for the next leg of our journey," said Tadis.

Baz settled into a routine as though he might stay in the village forever. Mornings he would practice his tricks. In the afternoon he helped Barrel with the wood or collected the dry grass that grew in clumps beside the dirt paths among the village houses. He did this for Tadis, who sat in the shade fashioning small figures. He wove them from straw and dried grass and strung them together, and they would begin to dance. Then he would sell them.

"When I have made enough, we will leave," he said.

"When will that be?" asked Baz. He had begun to carve the figure of a horse from a scrap of wood. He liked the feel of shaping it, revealing what was in the wood. He could understand how his father felt when he did this work.

"I do not know," said Tadis. "But not yet."

In the evening Barrel would seek them out.

"Where have you come from?" he asked Baz one day. Baz repeated the name of his own village, but it had no meaning for the boy.

"How long have you been away?" asked Barrel.

"Weeks, maybe months," said Baz.

"And where are you going?" asked Barrel.

"Toward the mountains," said Baz, gazing off into the distance. The mountains did not seem so far, but by now he knew they were much farther than they looked.

Barrel's face clouded over. "You know what they say about those mountains?" His voice dropped to a whisper. "That deep within there are caves and tunnels that lead to the center of the earth. And people who find them and enter never again return."

"I don't believe we'll be going to the center of the earth," said Baz, who nonetheless had begun to feel unsettled.

That night he told Tadis what Barrel had told him. "He says that the mountains lead to the center of the earth. He says that people enter and never return."

"That is not Barrel speaking," said Tadis, who was thanking the earth for his luck, for his earnings, for his life, as he did at the close of each day.

"It is fear speaking. Fear of the unknown, of things bigger than ourselves. You must transform that fear if you hope to become a true magician."

"How?" asked Baz.

"By observing it," said Tadis. "You will see that it will change. All things do. Nothing stays the same. And that includes fear."

"I still don't think I want to travel to the center of the earth," said Baz.

"You don't have to," said Tadis. "But maybe the center of the earth is not what you think."

Baz hadn't considered this possibility. "But perhaps I still prefer what is known," he said at last.

"But that is an illusion, too," said Tadis. "If you look carefully you will see that what is known is always changing, just like everything else."

The next day Tadis finished his last string of dolls and hung them above a doorway. The dolls danced on the breezes. "Tomorrow we will leave," he said.

True to his word, the next morning they were up

with the sun, gathering together their few possessions, which always seemed to be changing. The things they'd left behind had been replaced by new acquisitions. Baz liked the idea of leaving something behind and taking on something new. It kept the circle going in a way that seemed right.

Baz had a colorful new scarf and a tin spoon and cup. He was leaving behind a tunic that he'd outgrown, two half-finished carvings, and friends. For he'd come to know many of the villagers.

Barrel came to see them off. He had two fat wax candles, which he offered to Baz. "I don't know where they came from but I know where they are going. To the mountains with you."

Baz took them hesitantly. "Thank you," he said.

"I am ashamed to take from Barrel," said Baz later. "He has much less than I do." Though Baz had few worldly possessions, he had his freedom, and that filled him with a sense of plenty.

"You must learn to take as well as give," said

Tadis. "And besides, you do not know what Barrel has."

"He has a job that makes him rise at five in the morning. He has tasks that keep him engaged all day."

"He wished to give you the candles and you were obliged to take them. That is movement. Movement is life."

Baz wished to give Barrel the carving of the pony he had done. So he put it beside the woodpile where Barrel would be sure to find it. It seemed that he did, after all, have some of his father's talent, and he was happy to share it.

"I must say goodbye to the horse with no name," said Baz. He fed the horse a cube of sugar and patted his mane. "I suppose what I should give you is a name," he said. He thought for a moment of what the village had meant to him. Truth was what came to mind. He'd learned some truths there about himself, about life.

"What if I call you Truth?" he said. The horse rubbed up against him contentedly. He seemed to like the name, and when they started off down the road, Truth followed them to the edge of the village and then stopped and watched until they were long out of sight.

❋ ❋ ❋

Every few miles the road branched off in one direction or another. But Tadis seemed sure of which way to go, never hesitating. Baz himself began to choose a route in his own mind and then test himself, seeing if it was the same road that Tadis had picked. To his amazement, it usually was. He kept up this game until the loose sandy earth gave way to a harder, denser terrain. The sparse vegetation became fuller and greener and they entered a small glade of plane trees. Each had been modeled by the wind, time, and the elements. Each one told a story.

"Each tree has reacted differently," said Tadis. "And therefore each looks different."

Baz was glad for that. He was thinking how boring the world would be if all plane trees were the same.

They moved beyond the glade, into an open space that was not far from the trees but not yet the hillside. A place of indecision where the land hadn't yet become one thing or another.

"This place feels good," said Baz.

"Yes," said Tadis. "It is not yet this or that. It's open to possibility. The forest is forest and the mountains are mountains but this in-between place is possibility."

"Can the mountains become forest?" asked Baz.

"Yes, and the forest can become mountains, because nothing is ever fixed. All things are changing."

❋ ❋ ❋

With dusk, it grew chilly, and Baz helped Tadis make a fire. He watched the flame leap up in a tall fine thread, then settle and fatten again. They ate seeds and dried fruit and drank from the gourd and Baz's new tin cup. When they'd finished Tadis sat before the fire and looked into it for a long time, until the flame seem to move with the motion of his eyes.

"How do you master the flame?" Baz wanted to know.

"I am not mastering the flame. The flame moves because I am one with it," said Tadis. "It is the law of Oneness again, which has always been in effect on the earth. It is as old as the earth itself. That is why you feel pain when you think about your friend and the little dog."

"You mean Dagar and Blink?" cried Baz, astonished. "How do you know about them?"

"You told me in your sleep," said Tadis.

Baz wondered how this could be true. "I talked in my sleep?" he asked. He couldn't remember that happening.

"You did," said Tadis. "And I listened."

"I felt sad about my friend, Dagar, and the dog, Blink. But the carpet master who whipped us seemed to feel nothing at all," said Baz. "Is he part of the Oneness, too?"

"He is," said Tadis. "But he doesn't see it because he's created illusions. Illusions of power, illusions of separateness."

"I guess those were his dreams," said Baz. "But how does one know the difference between a dream and an illusion?"

"An illusion is something that comes from without," said Tadis. "A dream comes from within. To know the difference you must listen."

"But the carpet master had a law of silence," said Baz. "We could not speak while we were weaving or else we would be whipped."

"That was an illusion, too," said Tadis. "Because true silence comes from within, not from without. And when that is reached, so will truth be. Then you will know your dreams and you may follow them."

"And when a person kills?" asked Baz. "Is that illusion, too?"

Tadis turned away from the fire and the flame softened, wavering back and forth in a gentle dance. "Each time a person kills he is killing a part of himself. Only he doesn't realize it. But he will someday, somehow. That is a law as well."

Baz thought of Blink. "I have killed," he said. "I did it to take the dog out of his suffering."

"That's another lesson, but we'll save that for another day," said Tadis, laying the blanket on the ground.

10

THEY AWOKE AS THE SUN WAS RISING. BAZ followed Tadis into the forest, pulling the cart, leaving Tadis free to walk with his arms by his sides. At first he had been afraid to take the cart, not wanting to appropriate something that wasn't his. But then it had seemed only natural that he should pull it part of the time.

Baz had begun to listen without realizing it. It

was not the kind of listening that happened when he forced himself, when he made an effort. It was a more passive form of being, in which the noises sounded different. The trees seemed to sigh or sometimes laugh, depending on the wind. Well, he reasoned, if the mountains had souls, then the trees must have them, too. There were grass snakes that slithered to the movements of the trees, and there were birds that sang ragged notes. Somewhere in back of all these noises was a quiet that came not from around him but from within him. It was silence, which Baz had grown to know, to desire even. With it came an indescribable feeling of peace.

The peace lasted until the bushes began to rustle and the trees creaked in warning.

Tadis put his finger to his lips but continued walking, careful not to slow his pace.

Baz felt his pulse quicken, knowing that they were moving toward a moment that was inevitable.

At last Tadis stopped and pulled Baz close to

him. Instead of fleeing the moment, he waited for
it to come to him. It came in the form of four men,
their heads covered, their faces wrapped in deep
brown scarves.

"Thieves," said Tadis quietly. He did not wait
for them to speak. "You want money. And what if I
have none?" he said playfully.

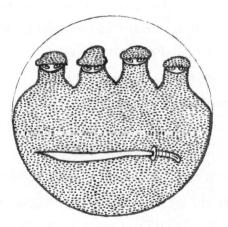

"Then we will take the boy," said one of them.
"I am afraid you cannot have the boy if he is not
willing to go with you," said Tadis.

The thief laughed. "Not willing?" Then he showed his sword. Baz saw that it was the sword that had once belonged to Tadis, that had been traded to the master for him.

"I know that sword," Baz whispered. He thought that perhaps this was his chance to turn back time, to trade himself for the sword. He let his mind wander to that possibility, and what it meant, but then he let go, realizing that there was no going back.

The thief raised the sword and it began to dance in a blazing arc, but it always fell short of its target.

The thief groaned, unable to make the sword obey his wishes.

"They will soon tire," said Tadis laughingly. And he was right. It was not long before the sword dropped to the ground. Tadis moved quickly, swooping it up. But he did not turn it on the thieves. Instead he reached under his tunic and produced a bag of coins that he tossed at their feet.

"I'm sure this sword has a price," he said.

The thieves grabbed the coins greedily and scatted.

"Desire again," said Tadis.

"You paid for your own sword," said Baz later.

"A fair trade," said Tadis.

"But they were thieves," said Baz.

"But I am not," said Tadis. He strapped the sword to his belt, the way it was the first day that Baz had seen him.

"The sword danced," Baz said with wonder. "Why is that?"

"The sword has my vibration," said Tadis. "It cannot harm me. But I did not hope to get it back."

"But the sword has a destiny, too," said Baz. "And I guess that's with you."

"For the time being," said Tadis, lifting the sleeve of his tunic. A thin stream of blood trickled down his arm.

"You're hurt," said Baz, startled by the sight of torn flesh.

"Yes, my sword has reminded me of my own

mortality." Tadis laughed again. He opened the cart and took from it a bottle of strong-smelling liquid. "Now I must ask for your help," he said.

"Gladly," said Baz. He cleaned the wound and dressed it in a square of cloth. He could feel Tadis's pain as though it were his own. And he now knew why this was. Oneness, he thought. Or at least something close to it.

Ahead a series of hills rolled outward and upward like a magical carpet, each a different shade of green. Nestled in the lap of one, they settled down to rest.

Baz nodded off instantly, exhausted by their travels and the morning's events. He woke a short time later to the sun high in the sky, but he was shivering despite the warm rays that bored into his skin. He turned to Tadis worried that he, too, might be cold, but Tadis was sleeping peacefully. When Tadis awakened he pressed his hand to Baz's forehead.

"You're hot," he said. He reached for the gourd filled with water and Baz drank eagerly, unable to quench his thirst. Then Tadis took a second bottle from his cart and sprinkled a few drops onto Baz's tongue. The liquid burned.

"It's the cold," said Tadis. "The cold has entered your body and it's now transformed to heat." He covered Baz with the blanket.

"But shouldn't we continue?" said Baz.

"We cannot travel now," said Tadis. "Besides, we're in no hurry."

"And destiny?" asked Baz.

"It is destiny that has willed this," said Tadis.

✸ ✸ ✸

Baz drifted into sleep, in and out of dreamlike chambers where he saw his life like pieces of a giant puzzle being put in place. There were his parents, his brothers, Dagar, the master, the man with no name. There were people that he had seen maybe only once in his lifetime and barely recalled. They were all reminding him of something that he could not fathom.

He awoke with a start. A kind face was hovering over him. It was a young man dressed in a tunic with a crimson belt. His hair had been blown by the wind, his skin browned by the sun to a beautiful nut brown shade. He poured a dense bitter liquid between Baz's lips.

"You are from my dream," said Baz, certain that he had seen the image before. "Who are you?"

"I have come to help you," said the man.

"How did you find me?" asked Baz.

The man smiled and placed cool cloths across the backs of Baz's wrist. "I did not find you. You found me," he said.

Baz turned to Tadis. "Am I going to die?" he asked.

"Someday you will die," said Tadis. "But not now."

Baz, reassured, fell back into sleep, this time

more restful. Every so often when he awoke, Tadis would put the gourd to his parched lips.

"I feel like the desert," Baz would say.

After two days the fever broke and Baz woke alert. He sat up. He could still taste the liquid he had been given by the visitor.

"I swear I saw my brother in a dream," he said. "Then he appeared and fed me a dark, bitter drink."

"Perhaps it was your brother," said Tadis. "And it was not a dream."

"If the man had been my brother he would have recognized me. He has been gone for several years, but I am the same."

"You are not the same," said Tadis. "I promise you that. Your brother is not the same boy who left home either. You are not the same as the boy I bought with the sword. Remember, Baz, that man took the sword because of desire. I let him have it because of desire, too."

"Why did you want me?" asked Baz.

"Because I saw you in a dream. You are not the only one to have dreams. I saw the potential of mankind in you, its capacity to love and forgive. I saw in you probability."

"How could you be sure it was me?" asked Baz.

Tadis pointed toward his heart. "A voice told me," he said.

Baz knew he was referring to his own voice, that inner knowing that he himself was just beginning to understand.

Baz reached into his pockets. The master's key, which he'd kept so close, was no longer there. His heart sank. Had he lost it? Had someone taken it? Perhaps it was one of the thieves, or the man who had helped him?

"I have lost something that wasn't mine to begin with," Baz confessed.

"And what is that?" asked Tadis.

"A key," said Baz. "I found it on the ground in my master's workplace one day and I picked it up. And I've been carrying it ever since."

Tadis did not seem in the least disturbed.

"Maybe I should have given it to the master," said Baz.

"But perhaps it wasn't his either," said Tadis.

"Well, in that case I'm glad I kept it," said Baz, laughing.

Tadis laughed, too, and Baz ceased to think about the key. It also had a destiny, and if it was gone it was no longer his. Baz relaxed into this thought. In his other pocket were some coins that he had not remembered having. "How did these get here?" he asked.

Tadis shrugged. "A trick of the magician," he said.

Baz drank eagerly from the gourd. He thought how his own thirst could consume him. Then he thought how any impulse could consume a person.

"How does one temper thirst?" he asked Tadis.

"By mastering the elements," said Tadis. He named them: "Water, wood, fire, earth, and metal. That is how the world works. Water engenders wood.

Wood begets fire. Fire burns to earth. Earth creates metal. Metal gives way to water. And on it goes in a continuous cycle. All magicians must master the elements."

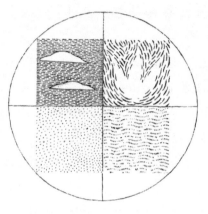

"I guess I must master them," said Baz.

"You have met with fire in the desert," said Tadis. "Wood you have met, too."

Baz thought of his father, and the carvings jumped to life like Tadis's grass dancers.

"Soon you will meet with water," said Tadis. He lit a fire and the flames mounted. Baz stared into the fire, too.

"I do not yet feel one with the flame," he said. "But maybe tomorrow."

"And tomorrow will become today," Tadis reminded him.

And they sat quietly, taking in the warmth of the fire until it burned out.

"Fire burns to earth," whispered Tadis.

✸ ✸ ✸

The road they walked on had settled comfortably into the earth, but because Baz was still weak they moved slowly. Baz had ceased to ask where they were going, ceased to long for their journey's end. His vision had changed, no longer fixed on his destination. Instead, he had begun to take pleasure in the actual task of getting there.

"We are all heading toward the same destination," Tadis said. "That is the least significant. What is most interesting is our journey. When you come to see this, then you've learned real magic."

Tadis stopped suddenly and turned to Baz. "Now you must choose a word," he said.

"A word?" said Baz.

"If you are to become a magician," said Tadis, "you need a single word that empowers you, a word that will be yours, one that evokes that which you wish to accomplish."

"Do you have a word?" asked Baz.

"All magicians have a word," said Tadis. "And it resonates with our vibration."

Baz wished to know what Tadis's word was, but at the same time did not want to ask. He smiled as he thought how life was often a series of contradictory desires.

"Is the word a secret?" asked Baz.

"No," said Tadis. "But it is yours and it will only work for you."

Baz thought for a moment, but nothing came to mind.

Tadis perceived his bafflement. "Like all things,

it will come to you when you stop searching," he said, laughing.

Baz laughed, too, thinking how often Tadis was right. His own notion of life had changed. What he did seemed secondary to what he learned. The tricks were important, but what each trick taught him was even more so.

They stopped to eat in the shade of an ancient tree whose trunk and branches bore the scars and dignity of decades. Some branches sloped gracefully earthward, and the higher ones spread toward heaven. Months ago Baz would not have paid attention to this tree or to what it meant. But now its majestic beauty filled him with wonder, and his word came to him effortlessly.

"*Wood*," he said. "That is my word. He thought of his own connection with wood through his family, his father, the very tree before him. Then he thought of *would*, the all-powerful sense of willing so necessary to the art of a magician.

"Wood has chosen me," he said.

"And that's worth a celebration," said Tadis.

They drank tea, which Tadis had reserved for special occasions, and savored sweet juicy figs with flatbread, which Tadis had wrapped in a cloth to keep moist.

Baz could not keep wood from his thoughts as they continued their journey. He looked at Tadis's hands, one pulling the cart, the other swinging at his side. They did not look like others he had known. He thought of his father's hands, lovingly coaxing wood into shape and form; his mother's hands, pulling weeds from the ground, working dough into bread; the weaver's hands, fashioning a world from nothing but thread. He looked at his own hands. Suddenly Tadis reached for one and Baz felt his grip and the energy of love flowing into him, coursing through his body.

"You carry a sword," said Baz. "But you don't fight, do you?"

"I do not fight as a soldier does," said Tadis. "War is separation. One must feel very alone to kill. The situation of being alone is terrible. It's not the destiny of mankind."

"But you are alone," said Baz. "You were alone when I met you."

"I am not alone," said Tadis. "You are not alone. No one is ever alone, because that is not the human condition. Each of us is unique, different. Yet we are all the same, all one. That is the greatest wisdom I can give you."

Baz tried to make sense of these words. "How can we be both different and the same?" he asked.

"If you try to reason that out in your head, you will fail," said Tadis. "It must be felt. And that is here." Tadis placed his hand on his heart as he so often did, and his sword danced merrily beneath his tunic, every so often catching a ray of sunlight, illuminating their way.

"Are you still going to teach me to use the sword?" asked Baz.

"Do you still wish to learn?" asked Tadis.

"Yes," said Baz.

Tadis unstrapped the sword from his waist and swung it into the air, crisscrossing his body. He thrust it forward, then pulled back.

Tadis handed Baz a stick and Baz copied the movement. From then on he would do this each day until the motions had become second nature, much like his breathing.

It was dusk before they came upon a village. They passed through the market, which was just closing, and purchased food and supplies for their journey. Baz stopped in front of a stall that sold colorful tunics and woven belts. Light cotton billowed in the breeze, and there was a man who sat cross-legged on a pillow sewing the soles to a pair of sandals. Baz looked at Tadis's bare feet.

"I will buy you a pair of shoes," offered Baz.

Tadis smiled. "No," he said, continuing on. "You need not pay me for saving your life. I was only guarding my possession. Don't forget that in you I am fulfilling my destiny, too. Often in life we need others to realize our own destinies."

That made sense to Baz. He thought back to the carpet, to Dagar, to little Blink. Maybe he'd needed them to realize his own destiny. That tempered his feelings of sadness. Perhaps in some unknown way they'd needed him.

"You must forgive yourself for killing the dog," said Tadis, reading Baz's mind. "You must forgive the master for harming your friend. And you must forgive your friend for dying, that is, if he is dead, because we do not know. In any case, in some unconscious way he has chosen his fate. Just as you have."

"Have I?" asked Baz, wondering how Tadis could know more about him than he did himself. "And what is that?"

"Now it is water," said Tadis, gazing into the distance.

Baz thought of Barrel's gift of the candles. Tadis had said he must accept them. Without another thought, Baz turned back and approached the man on the pillow. He bought a pair of shoes and offered them to Tadis. "You must take them," he said, "because I choose to give them to you."

"All right," said Tadis. He took the shoes willingly and packed them into his cart. "I will soon be needing them. Thank you."

They stopped to rest in a field of yellow flowers. On their petals were grains of sand that had blown all the way from the desert.

"They have traveled as we have," said Baz.

"Yes," said Tadis. "But has the sand followed us, or are we following the sand?"

Baz didn't know, but he suspected it was some of both. Anyway, it didn't really matter.

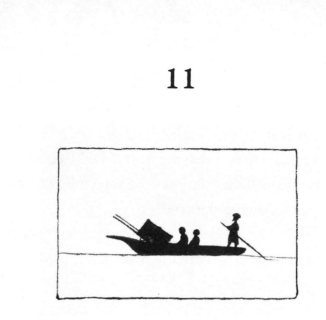

11

WHEN BAZ WAS SMALL THERE WAS A RIVER that ran along the edge of his village. It was shallow and he'd played there with his friends. He'd seen the water rise, swiftly taking things left along the shore and carrying them away. Then one day it took itself away. It dried up and was no more. Baz remembered this when he and Tadis came to a river. There were people along its banks washing clothes, collecting water, and transporting it.

"The water is giving them life," said Tadis. "And they are giving life to the water."

Baz and Tadis followed the river until it widened.

"We must cross," said Tadis, stopping at a landing.

A boatman was resting in a canvas chair, his arms flopped over his big belly.

"Cross where the water is willing," he said, laughing loudly.

"What does he mean?" asked Baz.

"I have spent my life on this water," said the boatman. "I cannot say that I know all there is to know, but I know where to take you across safely."

Baz stood on the riverbank gazing into the spinning currents of dark, swirling water. It looked treacherous, rocking the boat anchored to the landing. Baz was not sure he could give himself over to trust the boatman or the water.

"What are you waiting for?" the boatman teased. "The great flood? I cannot claim to know myself—that is an impossible task—but I do know the water."

The boatman stepped into the boat, reeling from one side to the other in a dance, falling into step with the movement, never losing his balance. He reached out his hands to take the cart, which he placed in the center of the boat.

"Come along now," he said. "Don't tarry."

Tadis climbed into the boat and Baz followed, sinking to the floor and crossing his legs. The rocking of the boat reminded him of the earthquake and the unpredictable shifting of the land. "How do you have faith in something so uncertain?" he whispered to Tadis.

"Nothing is certain," said Tadis. "That is another illusion. You might just as well have faith in this water as in tomorrow."

The boatman nodded vigorously.

"If you are against the water you are two separate forces," said Tadis. "One has to win. You must join forces with the water and see what you can create."

"How do I do that?" asked Baz, eager to learn that trick.

"You must let go of your resistance," said Tadis. "What is the worst possible thing that could happen?"

"We will drown," said Baz angrily.

"Then that would be our destiny," said Tadis.

"I do not accept that destiny," said Baz.

"Then it's unlikely that you will drown," said Tadis.

Now the boatman was roaring with laughter as he turned the boat with an oar.

"Can you promise I won't drown?" asked Baz. He looked at the boatman. "Or that he won't either?"

"Magicians can promise nothing," said Tadis. "We deal with likelihood and probability. But I can say it is improbable."

Their banter turned into a little game, which Baz was now enjoying as much as the boatman. He had forgotten about the rocking and reeling of the boat, the water that splashed over the sides. He had let go of his fear and begun to relish the motion of the waves.

The boatman smiled to himself.

"This man is wise," he said, patting Baz on the back. "But the water is wise, too. There is wisdom in all of nature."

"Are you a magician, too?" asked Baz.

"We are all magicians," said the boatman, nodding. Then he returned to the task of getting them across the river. Baz settled back and watched as they rocked to-and-fro rhythmically, the water displaced by the oars and then folded back into itself in one continuous motion.

"I thank the river every day," the boatman said as they reached the other side. "All I know is because of it."

"I don't feel like I know the water yet," said Baz, standing up, striving to keep his balance.

"You must be patient," said Tadis.

Baz felt relief as he stepped onto the riverbank. He looked back at the water and his eye caught a shining metal object lying at the bottom, rippling beneath the waves. "My key," he cried. "How did it get there?"

"Perhaps you have given it to the water," said Tadis.

"I didn't give it to anyone or anything," said Baz. "I lost it, or it was stolen. But how will I get it back?"

"You may swim to the bottom if you must have it now," said Tadis. "Otherwise, you must wait until the water wishes to return it."

"And if it doesn't, then the key is no longer my destiny," said Baz. "Is that what you are saying?"

"Maybe the key's role in your destiny has been fulfilled," said Tadis.

"But I don't yet know what that is," said Baz.

Meanwhile the boatman had pulled his boat onto the shore and was dragging a long net across the bottom of the riverbed. When it came back up, there was the key buried in a sandy mound.

"Here is your key," said the boatman with a sparkle in his eye. "I guess it is not time for you to part."

"Thank you," said Baz, taking the key joyfully.

"So that is your key," said Tadis, laughing. "I know it well."

"How can you know it?" said Baz.

"Because it once belonged to the sword," said

Tadis, brushing aside a corner of his tunic. The sword peeked out from beneath. Tadis pushed back the tiny compartment in the handle. "You see?"

"You mean this key goes there?" asked Baz.

"It once was there," said Tadis. "But it was lost."

"Well, perhaps now it's come home," said Baz. "I think it's time I give it back to its owner," he added, holding up the key. He was speaking not only to Tadis but to the sword as well.

Tadis took the key and returned it to the compartment in the handle of the sword. "I guess for the time being you have come home," he said, causing Baz to wonder if Tadis would ever say the same words to him.

Tadis gave the boatman some coins, and as they left it began to rain, large warm drops that rolled off their skin.

"Another chance to know the water," said Tadis.

"I forgot to thank the water for restoring the key," said Baz.

"Here is your chance to do that now," said Tadis.

Baz reached out and cupped the raindrops in his hand, and he thanked the water again and again.

"Water is amazing," said Baz. "It can become steam, ice, and then liquid all over again."

"It is not more amazing than anything else. Water has the ability to transform itself," said Tadis. "As we all do."

"But it never really disappears, does it?" said Baz.

"It is the same with us," said Tadis. "But it moves back and leaves the stage to one of nature's other players."

❋ ❋ ❋

The mountains were very near now, their nearness no longer an illusion. Their gigantic feet moved under the earth, stretching out into the hills. Their peaks played hide-and-seek with the sun, creating large shadows that danced on the surface of the earth as the sun moved across the sky. And as day drew to a close, their shadows widened to encompass Baz and Tadis in a grand embrace.

Baz recalled what he had been told about the mountains, that many have tried to reach the top, but those who are not ready die trying. His eyes narrowed and his body contracted at the thought.

"Then so be it," said Tadis.

It was late afternoon when they arrived at the foot of the mountain. The sunset had painted vertical lines of color and shadow that crisscrossed the ground and the clusters of houses on the hillside and their grazing sheep. It looked to Baz as though the entire landscape was vibrating, trembling.

Baz could hear music coming from a flute, bouncing off the rooftops back into the streets. And there were voices, people gathered in a square. They were flocking around someone who had come to tell a story. Tadis and Baz joined them.

"Who is it?" Baz asked.

A woman turned to him, her eyes laughing, her cheeks flushed.

"It's the Poet," she said. "He's a storyteller and a musician. He passes our village twice a year. And since he's been doing so we are blessed with good fortune. There is always something that happens upon his leaving. And this is a place where nothing ever happens."

Baz smiled to himself. By now he had learned that this was not true. Something was always happening. People just didn't notice.

"What does he talk about?" asked Baz, straining his neck for a closer look. The Poet was young and dressed in a white tunic belted with rainbow-colored ribbons jingling with bells. He was telling them a story about an antelope.

When the Poet had finished, he turned and began to walk away, the crowd following, singing to the chiming of his belt.

"Where does he go?" Baz asked one of the crowd. "Where does he live?"

"He is a wanderer," said the stranger. "He travels from village to village. He writes his poems on the road and he reads them to whomever he meets. He touches us here." The stranger pointed to his heart. "He has a mysterious and wonderful power. Tomorrow we will see that something has occurred. It will be because of him."

"He has been to the top of the mountain," said another. "His gift was given to him there."

"But who gave him his gift?" asked Baz.

"No one knows," said another.

"Does no one know anything?" Baz said with a laugh.

"None of us knows much," said Tadis, smiling. Baz had almost forgotten the presence of the magician. He looked around him. The villagers had fallen away like berries from a vine as the Poet disappeared into the hills, moving toward the mountains, which rose on three sides of the village.

Tadis and Baz stopped at an inn. The innkeeper was friendly but grim. He was used to people passing on their way up the mountain and he would warn them that the journey to the top was treacherous.

"Some never return," he said to Baz. But he did not tell him that he'd never had the power to change the minds of those determined to find their way.

"Tomorrow we shall see what has changed in this town," said Baz. "I wonder what it will be."

They woke to the sun shining down on them. The innkeeper's wife made them breakfast and they ate heartily. The mountain air had played with their appetites.

In the night a pear tree had flowered, sprouting white and pink blossoms.

"It is nothing that would not have happened any-way," said Baz.

"But maybe no one would have noticed," said Tadis. "The Poet has opened their eyes. He has made them see what is there. That is his power."

＊ ＊ ＊

Tadis took what he needed from his cart, food and warm clothing, and left the cart at the foot of the mountain. At first it was easy, climbing the low, flowering slopes. There were shepherds and farmers who offered them refuge, making a living off of people who wished to reach the summit.

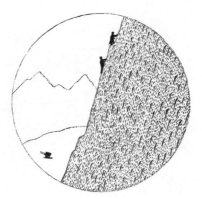

Baz thought about how the mountains were made. Long ago they were in the deepest part of the earth, somewhere that had never seen light, except for perhaps the deep fire burning at the earth's core. But then the shifting of the land had thrust the earth upward toward the sun. Baz imagined how the mountains must have stared in wonder as they met the light of day. And he could see how, yes, they must have a soul.

As Baz climbed he began to notice a pale white outline that followed the mountain's shape. He would see the same thing around trees and rocks. Sometimes the outline was not white, but colored, and often it seemed to be pulsating.

"My eyes are playing tricks on me," said Baz.

"They were playing tricks before. Now they are opening," said Tadis. "Let them open."

But as he walked and darkness descended, Baz's vision dimmed. The beauty of the mountain became harsh, rough. From close up the raw rockface looked ugly. Birds Baz had never heard before screeched, and he imagined them with giant wingspans and grating claws, shouting out warnings.

The mountain was steep in places, and every boulder became an imaginary beast capable of swallowing Baz in one gulp.

"They say that some of those who failed to reach the top fell into deep ravines, and others were swallowed by monsters and demons," said Baz.

"The monsters and demons were of their own making," said Tadis. "If you invent them, you will have to slay them. That is common practice, is it not? We invent monsters so we will have something to slay. Then we punish ourselves for not being up to the task. In this way we all make magic. But that is not what a magician does. You must surrender your fear of the unknown, of demons."

"But what if I die?" said Baz.

"Now you are looking your fear in the face," said Tadis. "And what do you see?"

Baz stopped to reflect. At first he saw blackness and nothingness, much like the view from parts of the rockface. Then Tadis spoke, and with his words a greater truth surfaced. "One can destroy the body, but no one can destroy the soul. That is eternal. And it will come around again and again until it finds what it's seeking. The earth will move, people will be born and die, storms will come and go, but it is the soul of all things that vibrates in a never-ending dance of light."

"You have been to the top of the mountain," Baz said.

"Yes," said Tadis. "And that is where I met my soul, that part of me not conditioned by mind, judgment, or perception, that part of me here."

Baz did not wait for Tadis, but reached out and placed his own hand on Tadis's heart. Then he put the other on his own.

They stopped to rest and Tadis lit a fire. Baz held his hands over the flames and the magician began to describe how the journey up the mountain had been for him.

"I saw fear and death and hunger and cold and all those things that every human knows. I tried all the tricks of my trade to manifest all I was lacking— food, warmth, company. I was by myself and I felt loneliness. Only when I thought I would die was I ready to give myself up because I was tired of suffering. And when this happened, I felt the warmth little by little return to my body. And I continued on, pushed by a knowledge that my destiny was at the top. I walked until my shoes were threadbare and there was no barrier between my feet and the earth, until I felt I was no longer distinguishable from the soil. When I passed my brother or my enemy, I was no longer distinguishable from him. And when I stood by the river and my tears fell, they were no longer distinguishable from the water that flowed along its banks."

Baz listened in wonder. He closed his eyes, and suddenly it seemed that the clouds were no longer above his head but inside him, white lights coming and going. When he opened his eyes the images before him shimmered and moved into the distance, until he was surrounded by a giant orb of space that grew larger and larger until the images merged, then fell away, and there was nothing but a deep silence.

"What is happening?" asked Baz. "I have never known such quiet."

"Silence does not come," said Tadis. "It is always there. You are simply aware of it."

Baz slept fitfully that night, dreaming of darkness and demons. But when he woke he fixed his eyes ahead of him until he could feel the stillness and hear the silence.

12

DAY AND NIGHT BECAME RANDOM AGAIN AS they traveled. They would rest when they were tired, eat when they were hungry. Though the trail had been forged by many who had come before them, there were places where it was overgrown as if the earth wished to hide the route.

Sometimes when night fell the sky would cloud over, masking the stars and the moon. And the mountain folded in upon itself in quiet reflection.

"I have never known such darkness," said Baz, staring into the nothingness until his other senses took over. He could feel the presence of Tadis next to him, and his own presence, like never before. Then gradually his eyes began to make something out of the darkness. They were not demons or monsters, but the soft blues and violets of peace. When a bird cried, Baz cried back, wishing to make contact.

Halfway up the mountain they met a farmer. Baz had seen no one but Tadis for days, so his joy at seeing this person was immense. He immediately felt how much the farmer was like him. And how strange and wonderful that he should find himself on the same place in this great big earth with this other being. There must be a reason for it. But by now Baz had learned that he did not need to know what that was. He needed only to accept.

The farmer was born at the foot of the mountain and had been a peddler, traveling the world selling his wares, always bringing something new from one place to the next.

"What did you sell?" asked Baz.

"Spices, pots, tools, cloth, carpets, tea. Anything I could carry," said the farmer. "I liked to see the look on people's faces when I brought them something that they'd never seen before. And then I would find that they had something I didn't know, and I would take that somewhere else."

Baz smiled at the thought of him carrying wares from one part of the world to another in the same way the wind carried the sand from the desert. There was a motion to life, as well as the stillness. It was the one that made the other possible. Baz understood that now.

"Then when I went as far to the east as I could, I heard the stories of a people who had journeyed to the mountains, and into the center of the earth. It was said that one day they would return to the surface. So I came back home hoping to catch a glimpse of them."

"And did you?" asked Baz.

"Not yet," said the man. "But I haven't given up hope. I've decided to stay here. I bought myself this small farm and some animals. I like to think that the wind carried me here."

The farmer got up and moved toward the fire, where he'd been heating water for tea. He poured out the tea and served it with sweet biscuits and almond milk.

"I have never been to the very center of the earth," said Tadis.

"Do you want to go?" asked Baz.

"If that is my destiny I will gladly accept," said the magician.

❋ ❋ ❋

"I have never felt such cold," said Baz.

They had been working their way for several days up a straight, nearly vertical slope of the mountain. They'd layered themselves in clothing and the blankets they'd brought. And they climbed only when the sun shared its warmth. When the cold became unbearable they would stop and make a fire and sit with their bodies touching, sharing their own heat.

"I do not wish to give up now," said Baz. "But it seems we are being tricked."

"We are being tried," said Tadis. "It is part of the journey."

"And if the cold keeps us from reaching the top?" said Baz.

"The only thing keeping us from reaching the top is ourselves," said Tadis.

As Baz shivered he suffered not only for himself and Tadis because of the cold. But he suffered for his parents, his brothers, for Dagar, for the master whose road would be long and hard, for the man with no name, the woman who had lost her son.

Baz had not believed forgiveness was possible for the things that he'd seen. He did not believe it could happen, or be helpful. But now as he tried to pardon, tears came to his eyes and he felt an energy move through his body to his fingertips, dispelling the cold, making it tolerable. It was a warmth generated by feeling, letting go. And in the instant that followed he could forgive the deep, dark, cold mountainside and see it as his friend.

They traveled when they wished, sometimes stopping for days to contemplate a small piece of nature. When food was scarce, Baz rationed it until he felt hunger in every inch of his body. At first he grew weak, and his grumbling stomach reminded him of what it lacked. But then the hunger gave way to a lightness and strength.

One minute it would seem that they had arrived at the top. They would be standing on a grassy platform that stretched far and wide. But then they would continue on and the mountain would suddenly reach upward again and Baz would realize that his journey was not over.

"I wish I knew when this would end," said Baz.

"Real knowing is that wisdom and knowledge do not end," said Tadis. "They are infinite like all things. So don't ever think you are there. Infinity applies to all. You will never know all. I will never know all. To know this is to know all. And to accept this is wisdom."

Above the clouds they met birds that laid eggs for them, wheat that grew like arrows, small pools with fish that looked like darts. There were berries that grew on trees and roots for making tea. They appeared out of nowhere like desert mirages, but they were real.

The air was fine and pure as they moved ever higher. And as Baz looked around he saw the great beauty of which he was a part. He did not know how he could have been angry at the earth or at this mountain for its movements. He forgave them fully and wholly.

"What are you thinking?" Tadis asked.

"I'm hoping," said Baz. "I am allowed to hope, aren't I?"

"You are obliged to hope," said Tadis. "Hope will increase probability. Hope can move mountains. Hope is focused possibility."

"I am hoping that someday I will arrive at my destination," said Baz. For a long time he had thought that his destination was the top of the mountain. But now he knew better. It was all that came after. The top of the mountain was just a beginning.

"Your journey will take you home," said Tadis. "That is, back to yourself. Because that is where your home is."

Now Baz understood the desert guide and the boatman who had spent a lifetime doing the same thing. They had journeyed hundreds of miles only to return to themselves. He knew what the man meant who had told him that at the top of the mountain the Poet was given a gift. At the top of the mountain the Poet met himself. And he met his own heart, where the light was clearest and purest.

Baz looked down at his feet. He noticed that his shoes had worn away until they were mere parchment and he could feel the ground beneath his feet. He knew as the last threads wore away that he was nearing the top of the mountain.

Baz could not say what got him there, whether it was hope, love, destiny, forgiveness. Maybe it was all of them. He thought of the leaf that Tadis had launched into the air, the grains of sand that the wind blew, the mountains that spiraled around and around themselves, the water that flowed, the great and wondrous energy of the universe. There was no darkness at the top of the mountain, just bright, clear light. Immersed in this light, Baz saw his true destiny, what Tadis had been showing him all along.

What distinguished a person was not duty or obligation, but capacity to love.

* * *

At the top of the mountain night came, too, but it was brief and nowhere near as dark as at the bottom. Baz let his gaze follow the stars to where their paths no longer converged but went their separate ways.

"You will leave me now," said Baz to Tadis.

"I will continue my journey and you yours," said Tadis. "But I will hold you in my intention and my thoughts, knowing that we can never separate."

Baz knew the truth of this. He and Tadis were one as much as anything and everything else on this earth. Distance could not separate them.

"I was given my power by someone much like me," said Tadis. "It is the power to create, but with this came the obligation to teach. I shall give you the power to create, Baz, just as I have. But never forget that the real power is that which we all have sleeping in our souls. It is the power to remove illusions, to see and feel who we really are. It is the power to love and forgive."

Tadis took the sword from beneath his tunic and strapped it to Baz's waist.

"One day you will no longer need this," he said. "One day man will learn that he cannot live by the sword."

"And the key?" said Baz, sliding back the door of the compartment in the sword's handle.

"That is another story," laughed Tadis, and as he spoke a bird of wonder came to Baz and alit on his shoulder.

Baz stroked the bird's feathers. Then a cluster of nuts fell from a tree and rolled to a stop beside them. Water rose from the earth and found its way to them in a clear stream. And Baz felt one with everything around him.

"Thank you," he said to Tadis. "I wish I could give you something."

"You already have," said Tadis. "You have helped me fulfill my destiny. And for that I thank you."

Baz blessed his parents, his brothers, each of the elements. And he thanked Tadis again and again. He thanked the darkness and the light. Then he slept peacefully, like never before, wishing for but one thing: a new pair of shoes. When he woke in the morning they were there beside those he had given to Tadis.

Baz put the shoes on. Then he turned to Tadis, noticing the magician's wrinkles for the first time, the fine lines etched in his face. He was beautiful, but he was turning inward, preparing for the next season of his existence.

"It is nearly time to part ways," said Tadis.

Baz embraced the magician.

Tadis spoke. "There have always been, and there are now, those who have a mission to walk the earth. I bought you to become a warrior, and my mission is finished. You are a warrior, but not as you imagined or thought. You are now a warrior of light. Go into the world, Baz, and fulfill your true destiny."

13

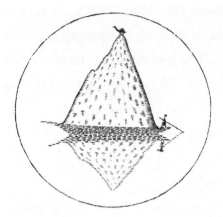

BAZ HAD BEEN WALKING FOR MONTHS, MAYBE years, crossing rivers and deserts with his cart, stopping to perform, watching the wonder on the faces of the people as he performed his magic. He witnessed not only joy and love but suffering and hatred. But he continued to practice forgiveness and gratitude. He would thank the earth, the heavens, and he would thank Tadis, for he knew that all were given the gift of life, but not the teachings that went with it.

Baz crossed the desert with a caravan and two guides. And he exchanged something with each person he met. If he had nothing, he gave them a smile, or a few words. These were the simple gestures of the magician. He met the boatman, who remembered him with a twinkle in his eye.

"So you made it to the top of the mountain," he said. "And now?"

"Now I have learned my trade and I must use it," said Baz, climbing into the boat and settling himself. He had no fear of the water as before.

❋ ❋ ❋

Baz sat beneath a tree on the outskirts of a village and stilled his mind and his thoughts. He had become skilled in this and all the things that Tadis had taught him. For three days Baz had dreamed of a young man, a carpet maker. But he did not know what to make of it. Across from him a man sat on a wooden bench eating a plate of fruit.

"Do you know of a carpet maker?" Baz asked him.

"There is only one carpet maker in this town," answered the man, gesturing toward the village but not bothering to look up from his plate. Baz smiled. Never had he seen such intent focused on food.

Baz thanked the man and continued on his way. When he entered the village he saw the flowers that he remembered so well; roses, jasmine, dahlias. Ahead was a small storefront. Inside carpets hung from the wall, more beautiful than anything Baz could have imagined. A young man came out to greet him, his face bathed in dust, his hands red with madder. But Baz would have known him anywhere. It was Dagar. The sadness in his eyes had been transformed into joy, but the long lovely fingers made for weaving were the same.

"Baz," cried Dagar, and the young men embraced.

"So I have not changed that much," said Baz.

"I would know my friend anywhere," said Dagar.

"I thought you had died," said Baz.

Dagar shook his head. "I escaped from the master," he said. "But I never stopped believing I would become a weaver. When I was sick and weak I saw visions in my mind and I held on to them in my heart. They unfolded like the story of my life and they told me my destiny. Even when I thought I might die I continued to weave my carpets in my head and the designs became ever clearer to me. Then I found, or was found—I still don't know which—by a true master, who taught me all he knew about weaving. And here I am." Dagar widened his arms to embrace his art. Baz could see that Dagar had woven his soul into his work.

"And what happened to the master who whipped you?" asked Baz.

"I don't know the whole story," said Dagar. "But I heard that the earth trembled. And the master ran from fear. He closed up the place and disappeared, leaving nothing but the blossoms growing and the fields of madder."

"Where did he go?" asked Baz.

"I've no idea," said Dagar, setting a small wooden table with tea and honey cakes. "But I have forgiven him. All that is past. So tell me about you."

Baz could see that his friend had learned much more than weaving.

"The master sold me for a sword," said Baz. "And I was apprenticed to a magician." Baz spoke with great love of Tadis and all he had learned. "That is my destiny. And now I am to fulfill it."

A little dog trotted over to greet Baz. It reminded him of Blink.

"That is my apprentice," said Dagar. "He never leaves my side."

Baz stood up and his tunic shifted, revealing the sword. As he opened his cart, wondering what he should leave for his friend, because he wanted to leave something, the key fell from the compartment of the sword.

Dagar picked it up. "And what is this?" he asked.

"It is the key I found," said Baz. "Do you remember?"

"Then it is worth something after all," said Dagar.

"I only know that it has passed through many hands and will pass through many more," said Baz. "It has its own journey and for now it looks like it is yours."

"But it belongs to the sword," said Dagar. "And the sword is yours."

"I have lost the key and it found its way back to me once. It will do so again if that is its destiny."

Dagar rolled up a rectangular square of woven carpet and put it in Baz's cart. "For your journey," he said. "It will keep you warm and bring you luck until we meet again."

"Until we meet again," said Baz.

14

BAZ'S MOTHER WAS IN THE GARDEN WHEN HE
returned. She had aged, her face lined and her body
slightly bent by the weight of years. But he saw her
as she was when he'd left. That was another trick
that the mind played. But then he realized what
that trick was trying to tell him. Despite how she
looked she was the same soul, the soul that connected him and brought him onto this earth through
love and creation.

She looked up. At first she did not know him. He had grown and his hair was shaved close to his head. His body was that of a man, taut and strong. But then she saw through his tunic.

"Baz," she cried, opening her arms.

His father was still carving. Little of his sight remained, but he had continued to work wood just as Tadis said he would. He did not need his eyes to sense the presence of his third son. He knew Baz by the sound of his footsteps. And he, too, spread his arms wide.

Baz's brothers had come home, too. To Baz's astonishment, they were the healer and the Poet from his own journey.

"So we meet again," said the healer, his eyes dancing with light.

"And again and again," added the Poet, embracing his brothers, for he knew that the circle of life would continue to bring them together no matter how far they journeyed across the earth, through life, and beyond.

That evening as the sun dropped lower in the sky, Baz pushed his cart into the village square. The people gathered, watching in wonder as he performed. Baz smiled as he thought of how he'd accused Tadis of fooling them with illusions. Now he knew better. The job of a true magician was to dispel illusions, to expand belief and remove the limitations that humanity put on itself.

In the distance Baz thought he could hear the notes of a far-off flute. He put his own wooden flute to his mouth and began to play. The wind rose and he was reminded of how the leaves, the water, the grains of sand, how all of nature moved to push us toward our destiny as a people. Beneath his tunic the sword began to dance and he thought of the key. It would go round and round, and in each person it touched it would open the door to understanding. And when the key had passed through all hands, as it one day would, the world would unite, and all would walk in love and light.

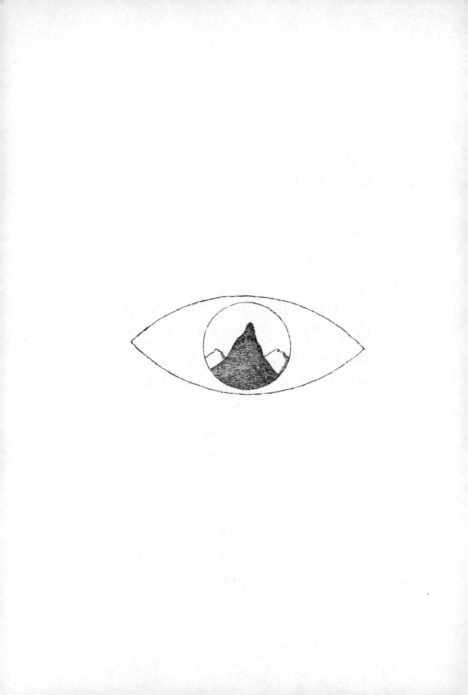